# A PORTUGUESE CHRISTMAS

JOSIE RIVIERA

# INTRODUCTION

To keep up on newly released ebooks, paperbacks, Large Print Paperbacks, audiobooks, as well as exclusive sales, sign up for Josie's Newsletter today.

As a thank you, I'll send you a Free PDF … The Beauty Of …

Josie's Newsletter

*Did you know that according to a Yale University study, people who read books live longer?*

*This book is dedicated to all my wonderful readers who have supported me every inch of the way.*
*THANK YOU!*

# PRAISE AND AWARDS

**USA TODAY bestselling author**

# 5 STAR READER REVIEWS

**Amazon Review by Liz**

**5.0 out of 5 stars**

"A Portuguese Christmas is a sweet and wholesome Holiday Romance by Josie Riviera. I loved this wonderful story and the characters, both were well developed. I was hooked at the start."

"Josie Riviera writes a beautiful, holiday love story while also sharing Portuguese traditions and information about olive growth and harvesting. Krystal, a talented American surfer who has suffered fear and injury, travels to Portugal for a competition but has no intention of staying. Can handsome, stubborn Adolfo convince her to stay? Find out in this delightful tale of love, loss, family and finding love again." - Amazon Reviewer

# CHAPTER 1

*I*t was simply the way it was in Portugal, another morning dawning so brilliantly. Dappled sunbeams reflected off the Atlantic Ocean; the surf pounded along a long, sweeping beach.

So this was a Portuguese December, Krystal Walters thought. It was so different from the cold weather battering her hometown of Newport, Rhode Island.

Here in Portugal, the sun never stopped shining.

She shaded her eyes, admiring the shimmering turquoise water. Feet snug in booties and reef socks, she wiggled her toes in the golden sand.

Hurray! Her anticipation grew with each breath of brisk, salty air. After a grueling year-long championship tour, the World Surf League ranked her as one of the top seventeen women surfers in the world. She actually stood on Medão Grande Beach's shoreline in Peniche, Portugal.

She tucked her waxed surfboard under her arm, hoisted her belongings, and headed for the competitor's area to check out the scheduled surf heats. Earlier that morning, she'd showered at the Oasis, an inexpensive hotel, and surfed for a short while. She'd encountered a sizeable wave and had spent a few seconds underwater. An hour had passed, and she still felt winded.

*Shake it off.*

Nothing would stop her, certainly not a little time underwater.

She gripped her water bottle, drained the contents, and refilled.

Slinging her lucky striped beach towel over her shoulder, she regarded the panoramic view of sky, tidal channels and mountains.

*I wish you were here to see all this, Ernie.*

A scream of sorrow slammed into her chest. Her carefree marriage to Ernie had lasted four months. And then, a week prior to their first Christmas together, he'd drowned while surfing.

"A huge wave will pack a big punch," the emergency medical responder had remarked. "Rip currents are drowning machines."

Ernie's death had left her disheartened. To escape a despair that never went away, she turned inward. Never again would she rely on anyone for emotional support. She couldn't bear the pain of loss, of abandonment, of defeat.

Sam Larson, an American surfer competing in the men's event, came to stand beside her. Playfully, he snatched her towel and dangled it in front of her. "Nervous?"

She seized her towel from him. "Absolutely."

"Ready to win?"

"I'm always out to achieve my personal best."

Sam nodded toward the voluptuous, sun-kissed brunette woman effortlessly riding a twelve-foot wave. "I gather from Wilhelmina's gutsy performance, she's aiming to win the preliminary competition too."

Krystal thoughtfully sipped from her water bottle. "She's an epic surfer."

"You're more proficient. Glad you're able to compete again. How long were you off the circuit?"

"Three years."

Sam's green-eyed gaze caught hers. The proverbial surfer dude, all bronzed skin and long, bleached-blond hair. "We missed you."

"Thanks." She swallowed the tightness in her throat and stowed the water bottle in her board bag. Affectionately, she patted her surfboard. "Angel and I are glad to be back."

"Angel?"

"My surfboard's name is Angel. You?"

"Umm, no. Although one of my buddies named his surfboard Rhino."

Krystal laughed. "I've always had a love affair with the ocean. I hope to generate a sponsorship from one of the swimsuit companies."

"Don't we all?" Sam smirked.

"Actually, lately, I've enjoyed sketching and designing swimsuits."

"Submit your designs. All the women's swimwear companies are represented here."

"Someday. For now, I'm here to surf."

Sam's smile was quick. "Conditions, swell models and the weather forecast are all textbook."

"Textbook is reassuring. I want to get out of Portugal as soon as possible."

"So you'll use all your feminine blonde, blue-eyed energy to accept your first-place winnings and leave this impressive climate behind?"

Krystal pulled sunblock from her purse and rubbed it on her nose and cheeks. "After the finals on December nineteenth, I'll return to Rhode Island."

"The purse is $15,000," Sam said.

"And if I win, I'm building an in-law apartment onto my bungalow so that my dad can live with me. We plan to celebrate Christmas together."

She was done with grief and heartache, and finally ready to celebrate the holidays again.

She scanned the spectators mobbing the shoreline, pleased to see her cousin Veronica, along with Veronica's husband, Clemente, and their twin six-year-old boys waving like mad cuckoo clocks in Krystal's direction. Veronica wore a wide-brimmed straw hat that covered her crimped auburn hair, a long rainbow-colored skirt, and pink floral scarf. Draped around her neck hung a camera and binoculars.

Krystal assumed her merriest smile and waved back. To cheer her on, they'd driven two hours from their olive farm in Évora. There was no reason for them to know her unease, or how much was at risk if she lost.

A tall man with thick, wavy black hair stood near Veronica. He crossed his tanned, muscular arms over his creased white shirt, and his worn denim jeans emphasized his fit physique. His expression was one of utter indifference to the entire competition—the crowd's lively applause, the announcer's incessant bullhorn, and the loud riffs of a guitarist strumming and singing that he wished all Portugal girls could be California girls.

Krystal studied the man's handsome features. No doubt he was Clemente's younger brother, Adolfo Silva. Although the men resembled each other, Clemente's softer, paler qualities suited his office environment, whereas Adolfo was tall and broad-shouldered, projecting an aloof strength.

Veronica had high praise for Adolfo. He worked the olive groves and consistently strove to build a more profitable farm.

How had Veronica persuaded her workaholic brother-in-law to attend a surfing competition? His stance was as rigid as a floorboard, a touch of arrogance in the set of his chiseled jaw. He glanced at his watch before bending to rescue one of the twin boys when the other hit him over the head with a beach ball. Adolfo muttered something and Veronica frowned, placing her freckled hands protectively on each boy's hair.

Under dark brows, Adolfo's gaze swept over Krystal, lingering on her form-fitting wetsuit.

Krystal felt her face heat. He was much too bold. Her wetsuit protected her body from the cold water. She wasn't a female specimen to be gawked at, as if she were wearing a skimpy bikini.

Haughtily, she met his stare.

His lips quirked.

Chin held high, she pivoted. She pegged him as one of those smooth-talking Mediterranean men who assumed any woman could be charmed by his lazy smile.

The announcer called her assigned heat.

She tucked the sunblock in her purse, secured the surfboard leash to her ankle and dismissed the fluttering in her stomach. Shaking out her hands, she tugged on her wetsuit gloves.

Sam clapped her shoulder. "See you on the nineteenth."

"Thanks. You'll surf great too." She snapped up her surfboard and quickened her pace to the water's edge.

An unexpected dizziness made her pause.

*Ignore it.*

She paddled into the cool waters while the head judge declared her wave priority. Krystal chose a large, walled wave that allowed her to gather plenty of speed, and she quickly reached the wave's velocity.

Within a second, she mounted her board and rode the twelve-foot crest. The sun on her face, the water around her, the natural movement of the ocean waves beneath her feet—this was her world.

The judges assessed swiftness, athletic power and flow. She was adept at a variety of difficult maneuvers and planned to perform them.

Yes, there were risks. And dangers. And consequences.

At the top of the wave, she stayed low and widened her stance to prepare for takeoff. She'd launch into the air, rotate and drop back down into the same wave. The key was to stay focused.

"Naive interference!" a man's voice from the milling spectators called out.

Her concentration broke for a beat. Another surfer took off on the inside of the wave directly in front of her. Krystal had the right of way, and this unexpected surfer was snaking.

She positioned to change direction, and a sudden steep wave barreled straight for her.

*Losing control ... losing control of the board.*

As she was sucked under, the water's force gripped her body in an unforgiving embrace. Nearly exploding in her chest, her heartbeat raced.

*"A huge wave will pack a big punch."*

*Stay calm. Don't panic.*

She curled into a fetal position, her elbows shielding her face, bracing for the imminent body slam sure to follow.

# CHAPTER 2

*K*rystal clung to the edges of her surfboard and gathered a strong, brave breath.

*Look up.*

*I can't.*

*You're a world-class surfer. You can. You must.*

A wave with a fourteen-foot face bore down on her, its force the same as if her body were being hit by a sledgehammer.

A quick surge of dread tightened the muscles in her legs.

*Paddle. Hard. Get through the lip of the wave.*

She thrust her board to the side and dove under the water.

Breakers flung her toward a reef and protruding rocks.

She gulped, tried to break the collision. Her right wrist twisted.

She was little more than a rag doll being tossed about while her surfboard was sucked under. *No, please*, she prayed. Her ankle was attached to the board by the leash.

Too late. The wave released her board, which flew back at

her like a loose rubber band. A sickening crack sounded when the board connected with her head.

*Hold your breath.* She floundered, pushed her way to the surface, choking on a mouthful of ocean water.

*Paddle. Breathe. Paddle. Breathe.*

*Don't be frightened. You'll use up all your oxygen.*

Her lungs demanded air. She couldn't pull enough in.

Distant shouts resounded. She blinked, orienting herself toward the large group of people crowded together on the shore. Salt water burned her nostrils. Her eyes watered.

Lifeguards and surfers sprinted to the water's edge and yanked her out of the water, dragging her onto the beach. She attempted to get to her feet and stumbled. Her wrist hurt, her head pounded.

The twins were screaming as Clemente and Veronica tried to calm them. Sam hovered nearby.

Adolfo knelt beside Krystal, his fingers moving over her scalp. He grappled for a towel from one of the surfers and positioned it beneath her.

"Most likely, the surfboard slammed into her head," Sam was saying.

Adolfo ran his hands over Krystal's right wrist. "Some swelling already." His voice was composed, his manner soothing. She didn't recognize his next words. He must be speaking Portuguese.

Veronica angled above Krystal, her slim red brows drawing together. "We're taking you to the ER immediately."

Krystal groaned through the pain. She couldn't afford a hospital visit, seeing that every cent was necessary for her father's in-law apartment.

No words came. *Please, please no.*

# CHAPTER 3

*K*rystal jolted awake when her body swerved forward.

Her eyes flew open. She sat in the passenger seat of a dusty red pickup truck bouncing along a dirt road, while Adolfo negotiated a hairpin curve. He drove dangerously fast considering the twists and bends in the road.

Disoriented, she peered down. A makeshift splint kept her wrist immobile. She wore a pair of royal-blue joggers and her black-and-yellow competition swim jersey. Her seat-belt was fastened, a downy fatigue-green jacket draped over her shoulders.

"Welcome back to Portugal," he said.

"Was I …" Her tongue. Oh, it was so thick she scarcely managed words. "Was I unconscious long?"

"A few minutes. Veronica helped you change your clothes at the car park. Do you remember?"

"No." The memory of the terrifying wipeout came back in a rush. She gasped. "I must return to—"

"We're heading to the hospital."

She stole a peek at Adolfo's sharp, angled profile. "I said I must—"

"And I said we're heading to the hospital, which is in the opposite direction of the beach." He glanced at her, his liquid-brown eyes filled with concern. "You've been through a lot and need to be examined."

Her brain—surely it was rattling inside her head.

"Don't think, just breathe, and I'll breathe with you."

In and out, in and out, she matched his rhythm.

The truck whizzed past orange trees heavy with ripe fruit. Acres and acres. And poinsettia trees in full bloom, the flaming red bracts set against the backdrop of an uninterrupted blue sky.

She licked her dry lips. "Where are we exactly?"

"I'm taking a quicker route to the Peniche Medical Center to save time. Veronica, Clemente, and their twins are in the car behind us."

"No hospital." Krystal tapped her trembling fingers together.

"I assure you our Portuguese doctors are as good as your American doctors."

"I can't afford …" The cost of a hospital exam in a foreign country was prohibitive without medical insurance.

"I'll cover any expenses."

"I don't take handouts."

"I'm driving, and it's a long hike back to the beach."

She was too weak to smile, to argue. In defiance of the blistering sun streaming through the car windows, she shivered and clutched the downy jacket more securely around her shoulders.

"All I brought with me," Adolfo explained.

She snuggled deeper, filling her nostrils with a pleasing, woodsy scent. "Your jacket reminds me of—"

"Olives." He kept his stare on the road. "I wear it on cold nights when I'm inspecting trees for pests and disease."

"How …?" At least her hands had stopped quivering. So many questions, none having to do with trees. She couldn't get a full sentence out.

"You'll be all right." Along with a reassuring smile, something flickered in his hazel eyes—hazel, flecked with gold. And the gold radiated compassion.

* * *

AFTER EXHAUSTIVE TESTS AND X-RAYS, Krystal waited for the results in a wood-paneled office in Peniche Medical Center. Veronica and Adolfo sat diagonally from her. Veronica's husband waited in the car with the twins.

"Bento and Bernardo might disrupt the entire hospital with their antics," Veronica explained.

"*Might* disrupt?" Adolfo asked. At Veronica's raised eyebrows, he added smoothly, "In all fairness, your twins are well-behaved when they're sleeping." He caught Krystal's gaze and mouthed, "When awake, they're terrors."

The humor vanished as soon as the examining physician, Dr. Dantas, marched into the office, his white coat flapping behind him. A distinguished man, he appeared to be in his mid-thirties, despite the stark-white streak down the middle of his black hair.

He greeted them with a brisk, "*Boa tarde*,"—Good afternoon—while he shook hands with each of them.

He sank into the chair behind his polished desk and reviewed a summary of Krystal's test findings. Peering over wire-rimmed reading glasses, he asked, "*Senhorita* Walters, do you play football?"

His English was stilted, the hint of a Portuguese accent

accentuating his distinctive rolled *r*'s and singsongy intonation.

"Never, I ..."

"My cousin doesn't play football, doctor," Veronica supplied.

Adolfo tapped his fingers on his thighs. "Instead of football, Krystal has chosen one of the most dangerous, frivolous sports in the world. She surfs for a living."

Other than a quick blink, Dr. Dantas kept his countenance blank. "*Senhorita,* these test results indicate your brain has experienced concussion on top of concussion."

Krystal didn't answer, holding the silence.

The doctor's dark gaze assumed knowing consideration. "You've hit your head several times throughout the years. Are you aware this happened?"

"It's to be expected. The sea is unpredictable and wipe-outs are normal."

"Some of your injuries may be micro-concussions."

"Micro means small, right?" Krystal wobbled to her feet. The room swayed and she gripped her fingers around the arms of the wooden chair to steady herself. "So when can I resume surfing?"

The doctor rubbed his black beard. "Not anytime soon."

"Don't concussions heal on their own?" She sat back too quickly and squinted against the mind-numbing thud in her head.

"*Sim.* Yes." Dr. Dantas angled to face her directly. "My question is, why risk additional brain trauma?"

"Surfing is my livelihood, and ..." Her benumbed brain refused to operate normally, begging for darkness in lieu of fluorescent overhead lights.

The doctor pushed back his heavy wooden chair and stood. "Give your body time to heal."

"For how long?"

"A few weeks, preferably forever."

She shook her head. "Out of the question."

"*Dotour* Dantas is not speaking Portuguese." Adolfo's voice vibrated with exasperation. "Are you listening to his excellent English? Your brain cannot tolerate any more jostling."

"Please Krystal, take it slow," Veronica broke in.

Dr. Dantas rubbed the middle of his forehead and briefly closed his eyes. "Do you suffer from migraines, *senhorita* Walters?"

"Thankfully, no."

He pulled out a pad and pen from the desk drawer and scribbled. "Just in case, I'll write you a prescription. Call my office if your headache symptoms become unbearable." He studied her wrist. "In spite of a bad sprain, we've ruled out a fracture and removed the splint. Ice your wrist every three to four hours for a couple days and keep it elevated and take an anti-inflammatory painkiller to reduce the soreness and swelling. Remember, rest is paramount."

"Thank you, although I can't rest.'" Her breath hitched. "The surfing finals are in a couple of weeks."

Veronica's hand shot to her throat. Her round, freckled face held alarm. "You won't be ready to surf again by then."

Krystal kept her manner steadfast and spoke directly to Dr. Dantas. "Once the finals are over, I'm headed back to America."

He ripped the prescription from the pad, retrieved a pamphlet from the drawer, and handed both to her. "With a concussion as severe as yours, plane travel isn't advised for at least six weeks. And no surfing, either. A second blow to your head could be fatal. I also suggest someone staying with you the next few nights, or until you are well."

The prescription and pamphlet slid from Krystal's grasp.

"My departure cannot be delayed. My father and I are celebrating Christmas together. I won't disappoint him."

"Your father can spend Christmas with your brother Julio in Newport," Veronica said, "and we'd love you to celebrate the holidays with us." She clasped her hands together. "On *consoada*, our Christmas Eve dinner, we'll boil *bacalhau*— salted cod—and attend midnight church service. My boys will be so excited."

"I can't."

"Of course you can. Clemente will send for your luggage at the Oasis Hotel. We own a small guest cottage on our olive farm. Aunt Edite stays there when she visits Évora at Christmastime, but she won't be arriving for a while yet. She's a freelance artist, extraordinarily successful, and manages our retail store."

Krystal lowered her head in her hands while reality invaded the doctor's office. A vow was a vow. Her father would never be alone. For the past three years, she'd been emotionally absent from him, from life. All this lost time, all those lost Christmases.

"What's wrong with staying in Portugal for Christmas?" Adolfo was asking.

Krystal shoved past him. "You don't understand. None of you understand."

Her father and her career were all that mattered, and Adolfo was concerned about her opinion of his eternally sunny country?

The office tilted. Her gait faltered.

Veronica came to Krystal's side, although Adolfo was faster.

Firmly, he held Krystal's arm. "In light of the fact that you can't walk farther than two feet without collapsing, it appears you'll be spending Christmas in Portugal whether you like it or not."

# CHAPTER 4

*T*wo hours later, rows and rows of olive trees perfectly spaced at twelve metres apart were illuminated by Adolfo's truck's headlights. He neared the cobbled driveway of his home, slowed, and almost wheeled in by habit. Set back from the road and sitting at the edge of the Silvas' olive farm, he could just see his tiled roof and marble porch.

His house dated back a century, and it was a former wine press. Ironic, considering his last argument with his father had been about grape vines and wine.

As he continued to the guest cottage, he pondered, once again, how Veronica had managed to talk him into attending a surfing competition. She'd assured he'd only be gone a few hours.

"A break after an exhausting harvest is necessary to recharge," she'd said.

Well, she'd certainly been wrong. Saving a woman he hardly knew from near disaster was definitely the opposite of recharging. He bit back an exasperated sigh at Krystal's single-minded insistence to surf again. Her slight form and delicate features contradicted her stubborn nature.

He parked his pickup in front of the white-washed guest cottage and eyed his passenger. "Wake up, Krystal. We're home."

She opened her eyes, fire in her gaze, a pout to her full lips. Belatedly, he realized that he'd used the wrong term. Portugal was his home, not hers.

He blew out a breath. She was certainly one plucky American.

The entire drive she'd slept off and on. That is, until she'd hoarsely requested he stop his truck on the side of the road. In the dry grassland, he'd held her silky hair back from her face, consoling her through long shudders as she vomited. Her gaze stayed downcast while he'd offered small drinks from the water bottle in her bag, and he'd gently wiped her chin with his handkerchief.

He'd never minded taking care of sick people. After his father was diagnosed with prostate cancer, he'd moved into his father's home to take care of him. They'd gotten along relatively well considering their many disagreements over the years—until the terrible argument that had severed their relationship.

A familiar knot formed in Adolfo's gut. He knew it well. Even after six months, losing his father was much more difficult than he'd anticipated.

He ran his gaze over his traveling companion, the blonde beauty who was once again sleeping. Somewhere, he'd read that a person suffering from a concussion should be kept awake for twenty minutes of each hour, or they'd risked falling into a coma. So, he'd roused her twice during their drive, discussing surfing, America, any subject he thought might interest her. In reply, she'd offered long-suffering side glances and hadn't spoken. A one-sided conversation wasn't his forte, so he'd switched on the radio, changing channels before choosing an upbeat Portuguese station.

He pulled his keys from the ignition. Twilight had faded to pitch-dark, the sky bathed in the light of a bright winter moon. Shadows lengthened, and the canopies of olive trees swayed slightly in the breeze.

A lamplight glowed within the guest cottage, the curtains tugged closed. He counted on Veronica stocking the kitchen with bread and crackers, food Krystal might be able to keep down.

He glanced at his cell phone. Veronica had texted that she'd unlocked the cottage and was at the main house preparing dinner. She'd stay overnight with Krystal after the twins went to sleep, and he relayed the information to Krystal.

He came around the truck, appreciatively sniffing the pervasive scent of olives. Why wouldn't Krystal want to spend Christmas in his idyllically scenic country? Portugal was the most spectacular country in the world.

He opened the passenger door and extended his hand. "We've arrived, *senhorita.*"

Krystal's long, dark lashes fluttered, and she surveyed him with drowsy eyes. She ignored his outstretched hand and stepped gingerly from the truck. "I can walk by myself."

He stayed beside her. "You're too worn out to venture more than a centimeter."

For speaking so abruptly, he chided himself. To say her entire day had been traumatic was an understatement. Compensating for his sharpness, he moderated his tone and slowed his pace. "Please allow me to assist you up the porch steps."

"Nope, I'm fine." She started forward and wavered.

*Sim,* sure she was. Automatically, he took hold of her arm. "Just in case, I've got you."

Once inside the tidy cottage, she used the bathroom. Afterward, he settled her in the living room on an L-shaped slipcovered sofa, positioned thick pillows behind her, and covered her with a cotton throw. Portuguese nights were cool in December, and he built a fire in the stone hearth.

He came to stand behind her. "Olive wood burns well without having to dry out first. You should enjoy a warm night."

She didn't answer. She hadn't heard, or wasn't listening.

"Care for something to eat?"

She sank back. "I should call my father."

Lightly, he patted her elbow. She jerked back.

*Loud and clear message received.*

He moved away. "Veronica contacted your father and brother. They're aware of what happened and will ring you come morning. So for tonight, eat and rest."

Krystal opened her mouth, a protest surely planted on her lips. Rather than waiting for her rebuttal, he took off for the kitchen. A countertop and stools separated the efficient, up-to-date galley from the living room. A one-light pendant hung above a white-tiled kitchen table and chairs.

He rummaged through well-stocked cabinets and found blue-flowered china plates and matching teacups. He hadn't stepped inside the cottage in years, and made a mental note to praise Veronica. She'd accomplished an amazing feat in updating the abandoned stone ruins into a modern, inviting home, complete with a wall-mounted television in the living room.

He hunted for food, pleased to find slices of just-roasted *pernil,* pork shoulder, in the refrigerator.

He set the teakettle on the stove to boil and prepared a toasted Portuguese roll with butter and jam for Krystal. For himself, he readied a crispy roll wrapped around the pork and a glass of red wine.

When he reentered the living room, Krystal was dozing. Firelight illuminated her wavy blonde hair, her flawless complexion, and small, turned-up nose dotted with freckles. Compared to his harsh outdoor life, she resembled a fresh-faced teenager.

Nearing the sofa, he fixed the tray on an antique wooden steamer trunk that doubled as a coffee table. "Your tea and toasted roll are ready."

"Thanks," she mumbled. She opened her eyes and gripped her hands together. "Staying awake is a battle, and my head is exploding."

"Very understandable." Rather than a clipped rejoinder about her dangerous profession, he took the polite approach. "Do you take sugar in your tea?"

"Yes. Sugar is my weakness."

"Good. I mixed in three teaspoons."

She accepted the steaming cup and proffered a listless smile. "Thanks."

He planted himself in a slipcovered chair across from her and swirled his glass of wine. As usual, his thoughts roamed to the farm and the daunting prospect of covering thirteen hectares of land.

"You don't seem to be enjoying yourself," Krystal said.

He glanced up. How long had she watched him?

"I get sidetracked thinking about the farm. Pruning is the next step after the harvest. It must be done hard and will kick-start the trees to produce."

"And I'm keeping you from your work."

He raised the glass of wine to his lips. "Come morning, I'll rise extra early to make up for today. Really, you're no bother."

"You're lying."

He shrugged slightly. *Sim.*

She smiled, a measured smile, much like the one she'd

given him at the beach. He hadn't meant to stare at her then, but her wetsuit had accentuated each enticing inch of her slim curves. She was an alluring woman, although she obviously hadn't appreciated his admiring gaze. He'd noted the proud lift of her chin, her natural grace when she'd swiveled and walked away.

He regarded her brewed tea and roll. "Eat. Take a bite at least."

"I'm not hungry." She propped her elbows on her knees. "Can I ask you something?"

*No.* "That depends on the subject."

"How can you tell Veronica's twins apart?"

He attempted to keep his expression straight. He hadn't expected that question. Goaded by the good humor in her voice, he said, "Bento is right-handed and Bernardo is left-handed."

A genuine smile burst across her face. "Suppose the boys aren't eating?"

"They're two growing boys with boundless energy. They're always eating."

Her laughter was infectious and he grinned. "In truth, I can't tell them apart since Veronica and Clemente carried the twins down the steps of the hospital six years ago." He took a bite of his sandwich. "More important than a set of unruly twins, how are you feeling?"

She eyeballed her swollen wrist and grimaced. "I'll be completely recovered in a couple days."

Her eyes were a strikingly crystal-blue. He wondered if anyone had ever told her that her eyes matched her name. Krystal.

He swallowed and got to his feet. "Let's take care of your wrist." He strode to the kitchen, nabbed ice from the freezer and wrapped it in a soft towel. Circling back to the living room, he asked, "Do you want to take anything for the soreness?"

"No, my tolerance for pain is high."

He elevated her wrist on a pillow. "I'm the opposite. A little discomfort and I gratefully take a painkiller."

"I can't stay in Portugal, you know."

"So you said." He relaxed on the armchair and stretched out his long legs. "Stay. Go. The decision is yours."

"Dad and I are celebrating Christmas together in Rhode Island."

"So you said."

"Dad raised me and my older brother, Julio. Did you know Julio was adopted from Portugal?"

"No, I didn't. Growing up, did you learn any Portuguese customs?" He didn't like the dark circles under her eyes, the paleness in her cheeks. If only she would drink some sugary tea, or chew on a corner of the roll.

"Dad was too busy working in a factory and raising us." Thankfully, she nibbled at her roll, singling out the crust. "He was a single father. My mother was never a part of our lives."

Adolfo wanted to ask why not, but Krystal wouldn't meet his gaze. He tossed down his wine. "So now you'll repay the favor by taking care of your father?"

"He had a minor stroke a few years ago which makes it difficult for him to live alone, although rehab services come in every day. Julio is recommending that our father live in the Lakewood Senior Lifestyle facility. He believes Dad will benefit from socialization and the activities geared toward people of retirement age." A heavy tone strained her voice. "I don't agree. Dad will be uncomfortable in a strange environment where he won't know anyone."

"And which option does your father prefer?"

"He stubbornly said he wants to live alone." Wistfully, she sighed. "I'm planning a traditional snowy New England

Christmas." She set her teacup between the wooden slats of the trunk. "Dad and I have become incredibly close, and we talk all the time."

"Become?"

"Yes, become."

"Weren't you and your father close before?"

"Excellent tactic, Adolfo." She tugged at the hemline of her joggers and sat back. "Ask me about my family as a diversion to stop me from thinking about surfing, right? What about your family?"

Her reproof brought an unwilling half smile to his lips, along with unexpected sadness. He picked up his empty glass and stared into it. "My father died six months ago. We never said much of anything to each other unless we were discussing olives." Abruptly, he picked up the plates, preparing to head for the kitchen and fix another sandwich.

A stifled sob and suspicious sniffle made him swerve.

Krystal was crying. Sighing, he set down the plates and settled beside her. He never was good around crying women. "Should I get your painkillers?"

"No, no." She dabbed at her luminous damp eyes with the sleeve of her jersey. "Now do you understand why I must return to Rhode Island?"

He fumbled. "Because of an olive farm discussion?"

"Because every minute with our parents is precious, and I won't regret another Christmas."

With a slight head shake, he watched the crackling flames dancing in the hearth. Sudden memories of his father flooded his senses, undeterred by his attempts to banish them to a safe, locked compartment in his mind. Alone, he'd gone to his father's grave at the cemetery numerous times, preferring to mourn in solitude.

He scraped a hand over his bristled jaw. "I wish I'd spent more meaningful time with my *pai*, my father, when he was alive. We argued a lot. He elected to grow olives exclusively, and wanted to someday press olive oil. When I was younger, I begged him to plant grape vines as well."

"Did he?"

"No."

"All the same, you went along with his bidding?"

"Of course. He owned the farm and I respected him, although we never sold olive oil. I was vocal about that. The oil business is so risky."

"Don't olive oil and olives go well together?"

"*Sim.*"

He and his father had held tightly to their opposing views. A silent dispute. No oil. No grapes.

She offered a comforting smile. "I admire you for respecting your father, and I'm genuinely sorry for your loss."

Her smile softened the rawness of grief over his father's death. "Thanks."

"My dad loves glazed ham and cornbread stuffing and I plan to prepare a four-course meal for him on Christmas Day. For an appetizer, I'll stuff celery with peanut butter—" A fresh torrent of tears slid down her cheeks as she spoke.

He never talked about his relationship with his father. In quieter moments, he reviewed the many times they'd shouted at each over the years, what they did to hide their emotions.

And now Krystal was sobbing about ham and cornbread stuffing and stuffed celery.

He fumbled in his pocket for a clean handkerchief and passed it to her. She accepted and curled up on the sofa, bare feet peeking beneath the cotton coverlet. She was gorgeous, reminding him of a model. Her photo should be plastered on the cover of an All-American magazine. However, surfing was a nontraditional, nontypical, and an extremely perilous career.

They sat mere inches apart. His fingers hesitated before he reached out to smooth sun-streaked strands from her wet face. Her high cheekbones were tinted a slight rose, the result of a morning spent under Portugal's freckling sun.

She cast off his hand. Still the spitfire.

Massaging his temples, he pushed up from the sofa and gathered the plates and flatware.

She wiped her eyes with his handkerchief. "I plan to compete in the Peniche finals."

"Remember your doctor's advice."

"He's not my doctor. Besides, he knows nothing about surfing."

"And evidently you know nothing about concussions. As long as you're recuperating on this farm, I will not allow you to surf."

"You won't *allow* me?" Slowly and deliberately, she placed the ice and dish towel on the table, then she threw his hand-kerchief on the trunk and came to her feet. "You've known me for what … eight hours?"

"And believe me, they've been a *long* eight hours."

"I'm sorry I'm such a burden." Her small hands balled into fists. "You can't comprehend how difficult these past three years—"

He set the plates and flatware back on the trunk. Again. "If you fancy being alive for the following three years and beyond, give up your freewheeling career and find something else to do."

She balked. Her eyes sparked. For a woman with a concussion, she came on full alert very quickly.

"And you won't be telling me what to do."

He gritted his teeth. Was nothing easy with this woman?

"When it comes to you risking your life, I most certainly will."

The entry door burst open.

"Here I am," Veronica called, her heeled footsteps tapping over the polished wood floors. "Bento and Bernardo were a little high-spirited tonight." She tottered into the kitchen carrying a sizeable wicker basket. "Bento helped me bake three dozen *biscoitos*. That is, biscotti cookies," she added for her cousin's benefit. "They're delicious dunked in a cup of hot tea." She plonked the basket on the countertop and laughed indulgently. "Bernardo preferred a game of tag, bolting around the kitchen table with his father in pursuit. Sometimes I think I'm raising three rambunctious boys rather than two."

Entering the living room, she stopped. Her gaze flew to Krystal's pronounced frown and the half-eaten roll. Then Veronica swiveled to meet Adolfo's scowl. "Am I interrupting something?"

"Not a thing," Adolfo replied.

"I told you to keep Krystal calm and quiet. Did you follow my instructions?"

"Every single word."

"Then why do you both look like you're contemplating murdering each other?"

# CHAPTER 5

Fanned by a temperate breeze, Krystal perched on a canary-yellow rocking chair on the guest cottage's front porch. Lightly, she pushed with her feet and rocked back and forth while waiting for Veronica's arrival. Green potted plants flourished in terra-cotta pots on the guest cottage's wooden steps.

Veronica planned a noon outing to see Évora's town square decorated for Christmas. She'd been so excited describing the festive city that Krystal had agreed to accompany her.

Black cotton slacks, a bell-sleeved navy blouse and comfortable leather loafers were the perfect choice, Krystal decided, smoothing her naturally wavy hair into a ponytail pulled tight at the crown.

She checked her wristwatch, squinting against the onslaught of another headache. "Not again," she whispered, willing the headache to go away. Falling back against the rocker, she pinched her lips together, seeking to come to grips with her frustration. Admittedly, her recuperation wasn't as quick as she'd anticipated. Her wrist still hurt, although the swelling was gone, the bruises faded. Her imagination? Possibly. Still, the burning sensation kept her awake at night.

Which was just as well. Her dreams were filled with flashbacks of her near-drowning, bringing her to a sweating, nauseating wakefulness.

*Avoid activities which may injure you again,* she'd read in the doctor's pamphlet before she'd shoved it into the bottom drawer of the bedroom bureau.

She shoved to her feet and took in the gnarled olive trees, the murmur of a creek nearby, the vivid purple carpet of lavender blooms, Portugal's national flower. Veronica's unceasing commentary about the numerous flowers native to Portugal—daffodils, sea daisies, and Portuguese squill— was a course in itself.

Brilliant sunlight sifted through the greenery of the old trees, the sky a cloudless denim-blue. Wilting in the heat, she shrugged off her red paisley tunic sweater.

It was all so picturesque, she debated slipping off her shoes and scampering barefoot in the grassland for the sheer, childlike enjoyment of it.

Since morning, she'd sketched ten new swimsuit designs. The creative process brought gratification, and the hours had sped by. And, she'd managed to blend ingredients for a round loaf of olive bread currently baking in the oven.

Olives, olives everywhere. The now-familiar scent oozed through the walls. Countless jars overran the kitchen cupboards, an outside container of glistening green olives was being brined for eating, and jammed olive barrels stood ready for the olives to be pressed for oil in the mill.

The previous evening, a World Surf League official had phoned, asking if she'd consider participating in the finals as a wildcard. The officials had taken into account the naive interference during her preliminary heat.

Her resultant injuries from the wipeout were being properly treated, she'd assured the official, and she fully intended to resume competing.

She wished that she could practice her surf maneuvers. A dozen times, she checked the global swell app on her phone for Peniche's latest surfing forecast.

The wipeout seemed as though it had occurred five weeks ago, not five days ago. Certain of her future, that her life was finally on track, she'd counted on a surf win.

Except that wasn't what had happened.

Instead, she was recuperating from a concussion and staying in a guest cottage in a Portuguese town she'd never heard of. And the town was located hours away from the Atlantic Ocean.

Twice, her father had phoned. He'd recommended basking in Portugal's sun, inasmuch as Newport's temperatures had sunk below freezing. Of course, she'd assured him of her arrival back in Rhode Island after the finals on December nineteenth. He hadn't replied, instead advising that she put all her efforts into getting better.

"Learn some Portuguese while you're there," he'd said, casually adding that he and Julio had scheduled a visit to the Lakewood Senior Lifestyle facility.

Surfing, always a prickly topic, especially after Ernie's death, wasn't broached beyond her mention of the finals. Her father hadn't asked further, and she hadn't wanted to worry him unnecessarily.

She wandered to the railing. Well past noon, and Veronica was late.

Veronica had married a Portuguese man and moved to his native land. With her inexhaustible good humor, the customs and language of a new culture had seemed an unproblematic adjustment for her. Most Portuguese spoke excellent English, the chief foreign language, she'd explained.

"All for the love of Clemente," Veronica joked, along with affection and commitment and a common bond of two adorable children. Veronica managed a household and the twin boys with ease, and she respected her husband. Chattering endlessly, she'd proven an enthusiastic caregiver, providing meals, tidying and tending to Krystal's injured wrist and occasional headaches.

Unlike Veronica's brother-in-law Adolfo.

Five days since Krystal's wipeout, and he hadn't bothered to stop by the cottage.

Veronica had mentioned the long hours involved in tree pruning, an insurmountable task for one person, even if that one person was Adolfo.

With a mischievous glint, Veronica had also elapsed into gushing detail on the number of times Adolfo had inquired about Krystal. Matchmaking was Veronica's specialty, so Krystal surmised that Veronica was spinning her own tales. Nonetheless, Krystal wasn't interested in dating, especially a man like Adolfo.

As the chat progressed, Veronica added that Adolfo didn't socialize as much as the eligible women in their area might like, and that he currently was seeing Isabel, who'd been a runner-up in a local beauty pageant years ago. Granted, Isabel seemed a current favorite with Adolfo, although many women, from Lisbon to Évora, competed for the possibility of being on his arm.

When Adolfo had stared at Krystal in her wetsuit, she'd assumed two things. First, he was a silver-tongued womanizer, followed by a close second—he had little else to do with his life than ogle women.

Right on the first part. He was a man who appreciated women, although she didn't know for certain if he was a womanizer.

Wrong on the second. The olive farm seemed to take precedence over everything else.

Something about his empathetic nature, the thoughtfulness that lay behind his strong features, disarmed her. Openly, she'd cried in front of him, something she'd never done in front of anyone. Granted, her emotions had been raw after the concussion, but she'd welcomed his soft tone and soothing gestures. Attentively and capably, he'd cared for her. Gently even.

Perhaps there was more to the man than his handsome, rugged exterior.

But while she'd been succumbing to her own emotions, that entire time they'd spent in the compressed confines of the cottage, Adolfo had seemed to suppress his own emotions behind a polite facade. Sure, he projected a quiet strength, an impressive appeal. Conversely, those attributes, combined with his intelligent hazel eyes, had little to do with his real attractiveness. He possessed an all-male way about him, combined with a silent barricade.

Perhaps that was why women found him so appealing. Adolfo Silva compelled women to find a way to penetrate his barricade, to temper him, to uncover what lay beneath his quiet, brooding exterior.

Krystal gave herself a firm mental shake. None of that barricade stuff mattered to her. One relationship in a lifetime was enough. All that mattered was winning the upcoming finals in order to afford her addition.

# CHAPTER 6

familiar pickup pulled into the dirt driveway. Adolfo emerged carrying a brilliant red poinsettia plant in one hand and a jug of pure, sparkling water in the other. Sunlight played across his good-looking face. His nose was crooked. Funny how she hadn't noticed that before.

He wore slim jeans and a charcoal-gray collared pullover with the tail out. His black hair was long and tousled, weeks past requiring a solid trim.

He smiled. *"Boa tarde, senhorita. Voca esta tao bonita."*

She lifted a brow. "I don't speak Portuguese."

"It means, you are beautiful." His smile, those words, caused an unexpected flurry in her chest.

"Do you use that line with all the women you know?"

His smile remained. "I've reserved it for foolish American surfers."

She ignored the barb. "Where's Veronica?"

"Chasing the disorderly duo around her garden. They got out of school at noon today." He bounded purposefully up the shallow stone steps. "How are you feeling? Your cheeks are still hollow and you're slightly pale."

"Thanks for the compliments."

"Sorry. I didn't mean—" He extended the poinsettia. "The trees grow throughout Portugal. Merry Christmas, or, as we say in Portuguese, *Boas Festas.*"

She didn't accept the plant. "What are you doing here?"

"I live a few miles up the road. By way of a bribe, I first brought the poinsettia to Veronica, hoping to coax her into feeding me a noon meal."

"So these flowers aren't technically for me? They're for Veronica?"

"Not anymore. Now they are for you." His grin beamed white against his tanned face. "She suggested I bring the flowers to you, and I took her advice." He edged open the door and sniffed. "Something smells good."

Krystal followed him inside and to the oven. The scent of homemade yeasty bread permeated the tidy cottage.

She tugged open the oven door, thankful the bread wasn't burnt. "I'm not a baker and scraped up two cups of flour when the recipe called for three. So for the third cup of dry ingredients, I substituted sugar. Being a master chef isn't at the top of my resume."

"Very enterprising. I'm impressed."

"At any rate, I prepared Veronica's recipe since the olives on the farm are rampant at reproducing."

"Welcome to a typical Portuguese olive farm." He stationed the jug of water and poinsettia plant on the kitchen counter. "Would you like a glass of spring water? I stopped at a stream." Without waiting for an answer, he brought two glasses from the cabinet and filled them.

"Water, sure. Flowers, no."

He twisted, the glasses in his hands. "Why not?"

She tested the bread for doneness and avoided his watchful gaze. "Flowers are too personal."

No man had ever given her flowers, not even Ernie.

Often, he'd tuck a gardenia in his own platinum blond hair, though.

"Well, the poinsettia wasn't for you. Does that make the plant more acceptable?" She glanced at Adolfo's persistent smile, uncertain how to refute the logic. He slid her a glass of water and dragged a stool to the counter. He drank quickly, set down the glass and wearily rubbed his fingers over the dark stubble covering his jaw. "My morning was difficult."

"I'm sorry."

"So accept the flowers."

"In view of your difficult morning?"

"In view of the fact I want you to have them." He successfully kept his expression bland, his voice insistent. Truly, the man was impossible.

"I can't. Flowers are too intimate."

He waved a dismissive hand. "Too intimate, too personal ... Poinsettias will give your cottage the first taste of Christmas."

"This isn't my cottage, and I won't be here for—"

He touched his calloused fingers to her mouth, silencing her protest.

He was a man who worked the land.

She was a woman who swam in the sea.

Flinching, she drew back. He dropped his hand and poured another glass of water. "The Portuguese word for yes is *sim*."

"What is the Portuguese word for no?"

"I forget."

She couldn't help chuckling out loud. "Okay, I'll accept them." She arranged the plant in the center of the chrome kitchen table. She was being churlish, and the flowers were wonderful.

"*Obrigado.*"

"I'm sorry?"

"*Obrigado* means thank you in Portuguese."

"Yes, of course. *Obrigado.*"

"Excellent. These are your Portuguese words for the day." He took up her swimsuit sketchbook she'd left on the kitchen table. "What's this?"

"Design and fashion are my passions. Except for surfing, of course."

"May I open it?"

"Sure. Why not?"

He thumbed through her pencil drawings of one-piece swimsuits designed for women of all body types and sporting a flirty, feminine appeal. "These are good. Really good. Personally, I prefer two-piece swimsuits on women."

She laughed. "I'm sure you do. Much as I appreciate your compliment, my sketches aren't good enough because I'm no artist."

"I can help. I've had experience sketching building models in my spare time. Does that count?"

"A building and a swimsuit are very different. Plus, I'm a perfectionist."

His gaze held hers. "So am I."

She gestured vaguely. "Someday, I hope to submit sketches to the major companies that specialize in surfing. Now I just need to come up with the perfect name."

"You will."

"My dream is to inspire the companies to develop swim-suits for the average woman, not pencil-thin models."

"Like you."

She shook her head. "I'm hardly a model."

"Ah, you underestimate yourself." He ran his fingers over the lines of the sketches. "What about your intention to professionally surf?"

"Even *I* know I can't compete forever."

He considered each drawing. "You're talented, and your

surfing knowledge will be beneficial as you develop these ideas."

"A prayer won't hurt, either."

"I will pray." He nodded. "And now, one more request."

"I'm not taking orders yet."

"I don't need a swimsuit. I never learned how to swim."

Her gaze narrowed. "Why not?"

"I never had the opportunity. The farm is a distance from the beaches."

"Swimming is easy."

"For you, *senhorita*." He grinned. "Now, if you will agree to accompany me, I'll show you my hometown of Évora. The city is quaint and also modern. Our town centre is partially enclosed by medieval walls."

*Surprise, surprise. He had an agenda besides the poinsettia.* "Aren't you busy pruning today?"

"I'm allowing myself a break. Besides, we'll only be gone a few hours."

She gestured toward the cooling bread. "What about my bread?"

"We will eat it another day."

*We.* She swore a male certainty showed in his grin.

"What about Veronica?"

He pressed back from the counter and carried his glass to the sink. "I reminded her that a restful outing is essential for your recovery, preferably without two wild boys let loose in the busy city streets."

Krystal took a long swallow of water. "Bento and Bernardo can't be as rambunctious as you claim. I love children and can't wait to meet them."

Adolfo made no attempt to stifle a laugh. "Be sure to wear your running shoes."

# CHAPTER 7

*A*dolfo parked his truck near Évora's town centre, still surprised that Krystal had actually agreed to accompany him. Even though he felt more than a nudge of guilt for neglecting the farm work, he wasn't immune to the delight that came from appreciating the company of a lovely woman, the delightful afternoon underscored by a rich blue sky, and showing off his thriving city to his most intriguing companion.

He opened the passenger door for her. "The biggest and best Christmas decorations are in the town square." Noting the dark smudges under her eyes, he swallowed an unexpected lump in his throat, a protective urge he hadn't anticipated.

He hesitated. "Are you comfortable covering the short distance on foot?" He could carry her, he supposed. Delightful thought, actually.

She tied the arms of her paisley tunic around her waist. "I'm ready and able."

He surveyed her tall, athletic figure. Her shiny hair,

reaching down her back, was pulled tightly off her heart-shaped face. Her unblemished skin was devoid of makeup.

Very nonchalantly, he attempted to capture her hand. Very politely, she refused.

He wouldn't push. He respected a woman's boundaries. She was too pretty and polished for a man like him, anyway, a farmer struggling to make ends meet.

As they toured the city, he explained the history behind Évora's medieval walls and monuments. She listened intently to his narration when he pointed out a prominent cathedral.

"I love historic cities," she said. "I wish I could spend days and days here." She tapped her index finger to her lips. "If only I had more time ..."

She didn't, he knew. She couldn't wait to leave Portugal.

He lapsed into silence and studied a modern building, analyzing how the structure fit into the older architecture of the city. He'd wanted to study architecture at university. He'd never had the chance.

They strolled across a stone bridge and down cobblestone streets until they entered the old town. Raucous shouts from street-market vendors selling Christmas wares punctuated the celebratory atmosphere. Tinned fish and tawny Portuguese wine mingled with scents of dark, rich espresso and *filhoses* made of fried pumpkin and dough.

Near the curb, Adolfo halted. "Do you like chocolate?" He nodded toward one of the vendors.

Krystal rolled her eyes. "You obviously don't know women as well as you think. Of course I like chocolate."

He paused. "Who said I knew women well?"

"Veronica."

With a wry smile, he shook his head.

They stopped at a vendor's stall laden with chocolate Santas, bells, and pinecones neatly stacked in rows.

"How can I choose between so many shapes?" Krystal mused.

"If you're here in Portugal long enough, you'll consume more candy than you ever imagined. We use chocolate to decorate our Christmas trees."

She slanted him a smile and went back to contemplating the chocolate.

"Pick one," he prompted.

She pointed to a chocolate bell.

"The beautiful *senhorita* and I will share a bell." Adolfo paid and handed the chocolate to Krystal.

They stepped out from beneath the stand's awning and into the sunny street, lingering on the corner, relishing bite after chocolate bite. In between licking their lips and dividing the chocolate, half a dozen friends hailed Adolfo with a friendly *"Feliz Natal."*

As they spoke in rapid Portuguese, numerous women nodded toward Krystal, hiding their inquisitiveness behind good-natured smiles. Their consideration changed to blatant speculation when they learned she was an American surfer occupying Veronica's guest cottage.

After the women left, Krystal asked, "'*Feliz Natal'* means Merry Christmas, right?"

"*Sim.*"

She wiped a chocolate smudge from her cheek. "And a couple of those women were your former girlfriends?"

"How did you know?"

"I could tell by the way they ogled you, and the way they pouted at me."

He didn't respond. Definitely, this beautiful woman was perceptive.

"The outdoor air will help your recovery." He considered smoothing a finger over the bloom of color appearing on her cheeks. Anticipating her response, he thought better of it and shoved his hands into his pockets. When it came to being touched, she was as jumpy as a newborn foal.

A towering Christmas tree greeted them when they entered the town square, and Krystal came to an abrupt halt. A slow, radiant smile worked its way across her face. The twelve-foot pine rose majestically, adorned in enormous clusters of silver, red, and green Christmas bulbs, illuminated by hundreds of tiny white lights.

"Are the Portuguese trying to outdo the Americans?" she teased. "These Christmas decorations are gorgeous."

He chuckled at her quip while he admired the relaxed elegance of her stance. Her black slacks and a navy blouse enhanced her lithe figure. Although sporting a casual pony-tail, she was a class act, carrying unassuming grace with ease.

He tried to decide what sort of Christmas outfit would complement her easy, natural style.

He shook his head. *What are you thinking? You'll never spend Christmas with her, escort her to Midnight Mass, Missa do Galo, or gather around the table for a traditional Christmas Eve dinner of codfish and boiled potatoes.*

He wouldn't be able to take her anywhere, for the holi-days or otherwise, ever.

Perhaps it was the way the rosy light of the afternoon sun enhanced her finely etched features or her easy-going smile. Regardless, the realization of her leave-taking left a surprising void in his chest.

He pushed the thought aside. He would accept the fact that she was here for a brief time, and not allow the thought of never seeing her again spoil an agreeable and memorable afternoon. And he would certainly never ask her to stay. Women required too much maintenance, and his life was here in Portugal, cultivating the farm. Hers was in America.

"Whoever drew that picture is very talented and creative." Krystal indicated a colorful crayon drawing.

"It is one of our many Portuguese traditions. School-children bring their artwork, and all decorations are welcome." He gestured to a particularly whimsical drawing. "We call the wise men from the Bible *Reis Magos*, so I taught you two more Portuguese words today."

Pinecones and homemade stars, and no fewer than twenty depictions of cows and donkeys, nestled amid an array of chocolate shapes and sparkling Christmas tree lights.

"Beautiful," she said. A few strands had loosened from her ponytail and framed her face. He resisted the urge to hook the strands behind her ears so he could better see the excitement shining from her captivating blue eyes.

"*Sim,*" he softly agreed.

She blushed and stepped away, navigating through the swarm of people, leaving him no choice but to follow her. Evidently, she didn't accept compliments well.

"Why is the city so busy on a weekday?" she asked when he caught up.

"As usual, there is a festival going on." He subtly navigated her to the perimeter of the crowd.

"A festival for what?"

"It doesn't matter. We use any excuse to celebrate an occasion. Today happens to be a local saint's feast."

A kaleidoscope of colorful dresses whirled past. The women wore eye-catching checked bouffant skirts and red scarves tied around their hair. Krystal watched the parade, but then she apparently caught the aroma of sizzling, crisp seafood floating through the air from an outdoor café. As her steps slowed, he guided her toward a wrought iron table and chairs situated on the sidewalk.

"Are you hungry?"

"A little. You forced me to share my chocolate bell, remember?"

He chuckled, drew out a seat for her, and accepted menus from a black-suited waiter. He sat opposite her and perused the menu. "Do you like fish?"

"I can eat almost anything. Surfing is a tough sport and uses up a lot of calories."

"Excellent. The Portuguese take long, leisurely lunches. Do you like grilled sardines?"

"I'm still recovering from queasiness, so I'll stick with coffee and dessert." She scanned the menu. "What do you suggest?"

He drew her attention to an image of a custard tart and grinned as she attempted to pronounce it: "*Pastel de nata.*"

He provided a thumbs-up and ordered two espresso coffees and three custard tarts, sprinkled with cinnamon and powdered sugar. He relaxed, entertained by the dance troops, the fancily decorated props, and the obligatory Portuguese celebrity holding up a sign advertising a bull fight.

The waiter set down their coffees and desserts.

Krystal eyed the prominent bullfight sign. "I've never seen a bullfight."

"It can be a fierce sport. Nonetheless, bullfighting is a well-established tradition." He scooped up a mouthful of pastry, smoothly changing the subject to something less violent. "In less than a week, a nativity will be set up, along with an ice skating rink and another marketplace. And then, we will have another festival."

She chuckled and polished off her pastry. "Is the third *pastel de nata* for me or for you?"

"We can share."

She opened her mouth, presumably to tell him he didn't share fairly. He'd eaten 90 percent of the chocolate Christmas bell.

"Adolfo, my good friend!"

Adolfo swung around at the booming, recognizable voice.

A full-bearded man wearing a black rumpled linen suit and smoking an ever-present cigar wended toward them.

"Francisco?" Slowly, Adolfo came to his feet. "What are you doing in Évora?"

"Early parole, old friend." The men exchanged Portuguese salutations and shook hands.

Francisco's mirrored aviator sunglasses kept his eyes hidden. *Convenient,* Adolfo thought. *He always had something to hide, especially as he grew into adulthood.*

Francisco plucked his sunglasses off and leveled a blatant gray-eyed stare at Krystal. "Who is this divine woman? An acquaintance of our mutual friend Isabel?"

Adolfo ignored Francisco's deliberate implication. They'd known Isabel since their teens, and news in a small city of less than 60,000 people certainly traveled fast. Unquestionably, Isabel was a striking woman. Be that as it may, he had tired of her seductive, throaty laugh, eager availability and avid interest in beauty pageants, which she helped to organize. She certainly didn't have a mind to talk business, which was why he'd called on her.

She didn't spar with him or challenge him, nor would she ever dream of leaving her house without makeup. She lacked something. A sparkle, a determination no matter the odds. She wasn't a splendid, willowy beauty. She wasn't … Krystal.

In the way of an introduction, Adolfo said, "Francisco, please meet Krystal, an American surfer."

"*Belissimo.* I am delighted, *senhorita.*" Francisco leaned in and kissed Krystal's hand.

She snatched her hand away.

"My country has miles of beaches," Francisco went on, "and I've always wanted to learn how to surf. Will you teach me?"

"I don't—"

He cut off her refusal. Francisco was always quick to try out all the angles. "How long are you in town, *senhorita?*"

"Only a few—"

"When were you released from prison, Francisco?" Adolfo interrupted.

"A week ago." Francisco tucked his sunglasses into a pocket of his emerald-green jacket. "My behavior was exemplary, because I know how to manipulate the system. Now I'm counting on finding employment somewhere. Is the olive harvest finished for the season?"

Adolfo inclined his head. "*Sim.* You've lived in Portugal long enough to know this."

"Will you ring me if you hear of any work?"

"Why? So now you are willing to toil in the fields?"

"Solely for a short while until I get on my feet financially. You know I'm experienced. How can I ever forget waking at dawn and sneaking port while I harvested olives on your farm? The wine helped steady my olive comb because your father was a hard taskmaster, constantly scolding everyone. Except Clemente—who was always studying for one test or another."

"No one wielded the pruning saw as well as my *pai*," Adolfo said softly.

Francisco's wolfish gaze landed on Krystal again.

Adolfo drummed his hands on his thighs. He might consider helping Francisco find work if Francisco could ever take his eyes off Krystal.

"At the end of a harvesting day," Francisco said, "I never knew on which terrace I left my olive rake." He slicked back a fringe of bleached hair. "Remember joyriding these streets in your souped-up truck? We attracted everyone's attention, especially one particular lady."

"*Sim.*"

"And the bonfires? We'd invite our friends from miles

around and secretly haul away empty kegs of beer before your parents woke. I can reveal many outrageous memories, my friend."

"I'm sure you can." Adolfo swore under his breath. "Keep them to yourself."

Often, Adolfo had wondered whether he and Francisco really were in agreement about anything, considering they weren't alike. Francisco was too irresponsible, too impetuous. Still, they'd boasted many a carefree day together in their youth.

"Let's reminisce over a bottle of port and a cigar," Francisco said.

A familiar flash of anger made Adolfo pause. "As you well know, I don't smoke."

"Of course you don't smoke," Francisco countered. "You're too taken with laboring over olive trees. Will you at least agree to sharing port with me?"

*Never at a loss for words, this guy, and wouldn't know how to respond to the word no if someone shouted it in his ear.*

Adolfo glanced at his wristwatch. "Certainly."

Stiffly, the men shook hands. Francisco blew a kiss over his shoulder at Krystal, then swaggered into the crowd.

"Who *was* that man—all dapper and charming?" Krystal asked.

Adolfo lowered himself back into his chair. "Try another question."

"Why?"

He pushed his espresso aside. "Because it's late and we should leave."

"What happened to our long and leisurely Portuguese lunch?"

"I changed my mind."

"Well, I haven't. Why won't you tell me more about Francisco?"

"I never knew you were so interested in ex-cons."

"He called you an old friend."

"As children, *sim*. We became rivals in our teens because of a woman."

"Is she the particular lady Francisco mentioned?"

"*Sim*. He pursued her relentlessly, and she wasn't interested." Adolfo tempered his tone. Francisco always knew what buttons to push to cause Adolfo's temper to flare. "As kids, we often dared each other to jump off the highest cliff or swim in the deepest streams."

She propped her elbows on the table. "Who won?"

"Whoever was the most reckless and fearless." He scrubbed a hand over his face, an attempt to wash away his and Francisco's foolhardy escapades. Where had those light-hearted days gone?

"Did you realize he was blatantly flirting with me?" she asked.

"Was he?"

"You know the answer. Is that why you don't want to talk about him? Are you jealous?"

He punted a stray stone near his shoe. "Absolutely not."

Her eyes sparkled, and she grinned, appearing a little too pleased by his denial. Her eyes reminded him of the Mediterranean Sea and the ocean she loved so much. A light, animated blue, darkening to navy when she grew angry. Her current shade, a blend of soft blue and softer turquoise, shone large and luminous.

In a tone of thinly veiled exasperation, he continued. "As we grew older, Francisco chose a different path from mine. His included rash decision-making. In contrast, the olive farm overrode everything in my life, including higher education. He earned an accounting degree at university. I staked and shaped trees, irrigated and fertilized." He fell silent, examining the espresso in his tiny cup.

"So, were you the most reckless and fearless?"

"Whatever the challenge, I won."

His *pai's* love had been conditional, based on Adolfo's achievements. His entire life he'd waited for parental praise, a positive *"muito bom"*—very good, very beautiful. Never, not once, was his father satisfied. Even Adolfo's mother couldn't please her husband, despite her attempts. Eventually, their marriage had become a polite, empty shell.

Krystal gazed at him over the rim of her cup and smiled.

Her whimsical smile warmed his insides. "Once I want something, I never give up."

She shifted her gaze, avoiding his stare. "If you're referring to me, to … us, I don't date."

"Thanks for the information."

Her statement didn't deter him. She was much too fascinating, much too appealing.

She sipped her espresso. "So why did Francisco go to prison?"

*Was persistence her middle name?*

"He did some creative accounting at his job and got caught. He had developed an expensive drug dependency along the way."

The biting, bitter aftertaste of the espresso prompted a grimace. She pushed away her still-full cup. "He seems charming."

"He is, especially with the ladies. I assume he's now clean and free from drugs."

"I hope he finds work." She toyed with the crumbs on her plate. "When he was in his midthirties, my brother's job was outsourced, and he was ultimately blamed for something he didn't do. For over a year he couldn't find employment. He and his wife were pointed toward divorce."

"What happened?"

"Long story with a happy ending. A private company

hired him." Distracted by a costumed bull with a giant head marching by, she abruptly asked, "What *is* that?"

"Judging by his popularity, he might be the same celebrity we saw earlier." Adolfo drained his espresso and eyed Krystal's cup.

She nodded. He downed hers in one swallow.

Krystal cleaned the crumbs on her plate with her fork. "My brother's current employer said that everyone deserves a second chance and that's why he hired Julio. Do you agree that everyone deserves a second chance?"

Adolfo folded his hands on the table. "No. Not when they are unreliable."

*There. Cool, quick and definite.* Despite what he was feeling, he'd honed the art of acting indifferent. But she didn't have to know that.

# CHAPTER 8

$\mathcal{U}$nder sultry skies, another two days passed, and Krystal worked on swimsuit sketches. She'd asked both Veronica and Adolfo if they would drive her to Peniche so that she could practice surfing for the upcoming competition.

Veronica pleaded busyness, and Adolfo simply refused, stating that the predicted heavy rains and a string of storms that might make the beach roads impassable. Although, from what Krystal had experienced thus far, it never rained in Portugal.

Perhaps it was for the best, though, because the thought of surfing incited her wrist to burn and ache, a phantom pain that was no longer caused by her injury.

The previous afternoon, she'd finally met Bento and Bernardo. The boys' constant activity had been a welcome distraction, and she learned the words to a Portuguese Christmas carol entitled, "Pinheiros do Natal," which meant Christmas Pine Trees. While translating, Veronica chopped garlic, onions and tomatoes in the kitchen for dinner, frying the mixture in fragrant olive oil while howling with glee at the twins' antics. Clemente had to work late, she'd added, and wouldn't be able to join them for dinner.

Later, the quartet assembled around the dining room table and snuck extra pieces of *coscorões*, fried dough described as angel wings. A snowman cookie jar sat in the center of the table.

Scrawled Christmas wish lists were displayed on the refrigerator, calling forth Krystal's childhood memories of bundling up in furry snow boots and thick woolen scarves, tramping through the snow. She and Julio would help their father cut down the most beautiful pine tree in Newport.

*Once. Long ago. When she was a child.*

Brightly colored wrapped packages were assembled under the tree on Christmas morning, the tags reading, "Your Christmas Angel loves you very much."

They were supposedly from her mother, but Krystal recognized her father's handwriting. Although her mother had died and loneliness had pervaded the household, Krystal's father tried to make every holiday magical. As the memories swelled in her, Krystal had had to dig for a tissue in her purse to dry her eyes. She owed him so much.

After she had devoured more *coscorões* than she could count, she'd been shown the Silva family's retail store located at the far end of the property. Soon, with the anticipated arrival of Aunt Edite, olives, tinned fish, and local holiday crafts would be sold there. The small store even had an old-fashioned, working cash register. Krystal could only surmise that a time-travel machine had seamlessly transported her back to the 1950's.

A day later, she still felt melancholy over her Christmas memories. She pushed aside her sketchbook and grabbed her cell phone. Since it was the weekend, she caught her brother at home. Their conversation went as well as their previous ones.

"Julio, please listen. You can't continue with your plans for Dad at the same time I'm held up here."

As she spoke, a violent gust of wind sucked in the white lace kitchen curtains. Captured by the wind, a loose shutter flapped against the wooden sideboards.

She peered outside. The early darkness was unusual, and a storm undoubtedly brewed. How had she not noticed this earlier? Little by little, a recognizable panic quickened in her veins. Ridiculous, this senseless fear of thunderstorms. She was a grown woman, closing in on thirty years old, no longer a youngster huddling in a closet with a flashlight. She refused to cower like a child anymore. She was a strong and capable adult.

Through her cell phone, her brother's transatlantic tirade made her blink.

"Please, Julio, don't make any decisions about the Senior Lifestyle facility until the surfing finals are over. I know Dad will be happier living with me." She grimaced at the thick band of clouds forming in the sky, and wiped her palms over her jeans. "Yes, I'm better and plan to surf in the finals."

Lightning flickered. She quickened her steps to the window and slammed it shut. "Of course you should visit Portugal someday. I wish we could trade places too, and I *am* appreciative I'm here. Yes, I know you work a full-time job, besides helping your wife care for three demanding kids—"

Her cell phone quit.

She stared at the blank screen and then pitched the phone onto the kitchen counter. No cell phone service? Now, the next thing to go wrong was a power loss.

She raced through the cottage in search of a flashlight, rifling through drawers and cabinets.

Thunder shook the walls like a cannon blast, and she was pitched into utter darkness a moment later.

Seeking refuge in a room with no windows, she scurried

to the bathroom and curled her fingers around the sink. She blamed her sudden dizziness on a rapid pulse, not the concussion. While rain lashed the cottage's exterior, she critically appraised her reflection in the mirror. A sheen of sweat coated her pale forehead and cheeks, in stark contradiction to her scarlet chiffon blouse.

The sound of a vehicle motivated her to sprint to the living room. Bracing her fingers on the windowsill, she scanned the vast acreage of the farm. Jagged streaks of silver lightning lit the sky. A gale wind howled, mercilessly bending tree branches as though they were twigs. Already, the dirt driveway was awash in mud.

Through the driving rain, a familiar red pickup truck parked near the front porch. An instant later, rapid, heavy footsteps echoed in her ears, followed by a firm knock on the door.

She opened the door, so thankful to see Adolfo she covered her mouth with her hands.

He carried an armful of large logs. "A menacing thunderstorm is underway," he joked.

Fat raindrops spattered against the roof, and she tipped an exaggerated peer heavenward. "You noticed?"

Resting one shoulder on the doorjamb, he smiled at her. His black hair, wet with rain, was plastered to his forehead. They were so close, she almost considered wiping away the beads of rain streaming down his rugged face.

"This is the part where you're supposed to invite me inside," he prompted.

Her heart did a surprising leap, which she attributed to relief at seeing him. "Yes, of course." She shook back the hair whipping across her cheeks. "Please come in."

He carried the logs to the fireplace and pulled off his jacket. She accepted the saturated jacket and hung it on a brass hook near the entry.

She inhaled. The same forest-like scent of olives, the same promise of his competent, reassuring presence. Gratitude pervaded her jumbled thoughts. She clearly remembered how, after leaving the hospital that first day, he'd treated her with compassion and patience when she'd become embarrassingly sick in the tall grass.

Across the width of the living room, he yanked off his muddy boots and set them near the hearth. When he got to his feet, his broad shoulders blocked her view of the fireplace, and all she could see was him. In worn denim jeans and a charcoal sweater, Adolfo Silva was the handsomest man she'd ever seen.

Fate had thrown them together, the circumstances out of their control. And despite her resolution to side-step romance, the R word, she was drawn to him.

He reached for the matches on the fieldstone mantel. "I stopped pruning when the storm neared and texted Veronica. She said you were alone, so I volunteered to stop by the cottage."

His baritone voice held the same captivating quality as when he'd cared for her on Medão Beach.

She fiddled with the cuffs of her blouse. "I'm grateful you came. The lights went out and I ... I ... couldn't find a flashlight."

"Out here, surrounded by pastures and farmland, we lose power often."

"Great. Just great."

His brows furrowed.

"What I mean is, I'm glad you're here," she said.

"I wouldn't expect a beautiful woman to sit in the dark by herself in the middle of a thunderstorm."

Beautiful was the only word that stuck. She was so pleased by his compliment that she didn't know how to respond. She dropped onto the sofa and rested her head on the pillows, her limbs limp after the thunderstorm scare. "Did you bring more olive wood?"

"Oak." He knelt by the hearth and lit the fire. The faint, soothing tang of wood smoke floated through the cottage.

"The other day, you mentioned olive wood burns well and would keep the cottage warm."

"And here I thought you hadn't been listening to me." He quirked a smile. "I brought oak logs to complement the poinsettia for the Christmas season."

She rubbed the base of her neck. "I'm sorry, I don't understand."

"On the days leading up to Christmas and throughout Christmas Day, Portuguese tradition dictates a piece of oak wood must be kept burning in every hearth. We refer to our Christmas log as *cepo de Natal*."

"I told you, I won't be here for—"

"In exchange for teaching you another Portuguese word and bringing you the Christmas log, can you get me a glass of port wine?"

Why couldn't he understand she wouldn't be in Portugal for Christmas?

"Can't you get your own wine?" she asked. "You know where the kitchen is."

"Of course. I thought you might—"

"Or at least ask and not demand?"

"My apologies, *senhorita*." He added a grim smile. "I didn't realize I asked so much."

His quiet, velvety tone had a disturbing effect on her pulse. She busied herself with tugging at the fringes of the pillows on the sofa.

"Krystal, look at me."

She hesitated. Reluctantly, she met his gaze.

"Thank you for coming to Portugal. Spending time with you brings me great joy."

Mesmerized by the huskiness in his voice, she felt her heartbeat quicken. "Thank *you* for coming to my rescue, not once, but twice."

"Much as I appreciate the credit, I, along with several others, took care of you on Medão Beach."

"You saw the storm and you're the one person who came today."

He suppressed a chuckle. "My exquisite *senhorita*, I will keep you safe from any storm."

"As long as I am here in Portugal?"

He strode to her, his gaze caressing her face, mouth, figure. He took her small hands into his large ones. "As long as you are anywhere."

She read his meaningful gaze, the silent invitation, and retreated. If she cared for someone again, loved again, she would get hurt, and she couldn't go through the heartbreak that came from losing someone. Her mother, her husband— all her close relationships ended badly.

She pulled from his grasp. "I'll go."

"*Abrigado.*" He lit a row of fat, stubby candles on the mantel, reducing the room to a soft, mellow glow. "We can wait out the storm and sit by the fireplace together, where we'll be warm and comfortable."

*Warm and comfortable, together, by the fireplace.*

Her mouth went too dry to respond.

Strategically, she routed around him and stepped into the kitchen. She poured his wine into a slender stemmed wine-glass, along with a glass of spring water for herself, stalling for time to gather her emotions.

Enthusiastically, he accepted the glass of port when she reappeared and set the bottle on the trunk.

"A toast." He lifted his glass and inclined her to do the same.

Spine erect, she seated herself on the sofa and held up her glass. "What are we celebrating?"

"The upcoming Christmas feasts, the fact you're here, and the fact it's raining, for the parched land desperately needs rain." He installed himself beside her, inches away. She snapped her head up, intending to launch into a discourse regarding his boldness to sit so near.

That is, until forked lightning sliced the sky in half, followed by a crack of thunder.

She set down her glass, settled back into the cushions, and pressed her elbows to her sides. He watched her with such intensity, she feigned absorption in the black metal corners of the trunk to avoid meeting his gaze.

"Are you all right?" he asked.

"I'm afraid of thunderstorms. Or rather, I used to be afraid of thunderstorms."

He lifted a dark brow. "You? Afraid? After watching you surf those huge waves like a pro, I assumed you were fearless."

She sat straighter. "You noticed?"

"Along with everyone else on Medão Grande Beach." His admiring grin reached all the way to his hazel gaze—brown or green depending on his moods. Currently, his eyes were an easy, hot-fudge brown.

She decided on a new direction. "I can tell them apart."

"Who?"

"Bento and Bernardo. Yesterday, I had a very lively day at Veronica's house."

"*Lively* is a good description."

"Have you noticed that Bento's hair is straight and a shade lighter than his brother's? Bernardo's hair sticks up in unmanageable swirls at the crown, and he's the inquisitive one."

"Never noticed. They're like two little clones of Clemente,

and both children are such chatterboxes, I can hardly think whenever they're around. Did you notice a minuscule mole on Bernardo's left cheek?"

She beamed. "Yes, indeed. You?"

He stared into his glass, muttering, "Never spotted anything remotely resembling a mole, although Veronica has tried to point it out to me many times."

Krystal smiled, but then she drank more water, allowing it to clear her throat in order to approach her next topic, one sure to turn Adolfo's affable gaze to a glowering, this-side-of furious green.

"Are you aware I'm completely recovered from my injuries?" she began brightly, holding out her arm. "My wrist doesn't hurt anymore."

Only in her imaginings, she told her intrusive conscience.

"Better," Adolfo answered with equal brightness. "Though slightly bruised, there isn't any more swelling."

"So … can you take me to the ocean this weekend? I must begin surfing again."

He tightened his fingers around his glass. "You know my opinion on this matter."

A charged silence glutted the room, interrupted by a deluge of rain pounding against the windows.

"The twins can come. They can build sand castles."

He seemed to be attempting to keep his temper in check. "I don't have time for sand castles."

"Veronica can use a break, and it gives you—us—a few hours away from the olive farm."

"No."

"Adolfo, please. I need the money, assuming I win. And I *will* win," she corrected. She never wanted to appear weak in his eyes. She'd done that once already.

He said nothing.

"My dad is planning to come live with me."

"We've been through this. You mean that *you* are planning for him to live with you."

"The completed addition will boast five-hundred square feet of living space for Dad."

"I know."

She shot him a murderous glare. "So why don't you understand my dilemma?"

"Does your father support your surfing ambitions?"

"For many years, I've supported myself."

"I don't mean financial. I mean emotional."

She rubbed her forehead. "In all honesty, no. In fact, he vehemently disapproves. He spouts statistics on why surfing's too dangerous. In spite of his opinions, though, he wants me happy, and surfing makes me happy."

"In our conversations, you've never mentioned your mother."

"My mom died shortly after I was born. I never knew her. I was the natural child and, as I told you, Julio was adopted from Portugal." She bent her head to hide the rush of sorrow filling her heart. "Perhaps—perhaps she died because of complications resulting from my birth."

"What on earth makes you say that?"

She kept her head down. "I've overheard whispers regarding my mother's hard labor. My birth might have been the reason she died."

*Oh, please. She'd said the words out loud. That made it real. She didn't want it to be real.*

"Has your father spoken to you about this?"

"Never. He's so nurturing. Perhaps he feared that telling was more than he thought I could endure."

She whispered tearfully, her words quiet fragments of pain, *I love you, Mom. Another lonesome Christmas without you. Even after all these years, I'm having such a hard time. I know Dad is too.*

Adolfo couldn't hear her, could he? She glanced up at him, worried. Those empathetic eyes. So intense, so attentive.

The room grew eerily still. No lightning. No thunder, the solitary tap-tap-tap of a persistent rain.

"I'm sorry," Adolfo said softly. "I don't know your father, although from what you've told me, he isn't the type of man who'd withhold information, no matter how distressing. I don't believe your birth had anything to do with your mother's passing."

"You weren't there. You don't know."

"Neither do you."

"I believe that my mother is watching over me—like an angel."

She had never admitted that to anyone. She couldn't take the words back, and if she could, where would the words go?

He waited, as if she might have more to say.

She sniffed and waved an airy hand. "My dad is wonderfully supportive, and I'm certain your parents urged you to pursue your dreams."

"Don't be so certain." He took a big swallow of port. "My parents were never satisfied with my work in the olive groves, especially my father. So the answer is no, they didn't. And no, he didn't. Happiness wasn't part of the Silva equation."

"Did you resent your father because of it?"

His jaw visibly tightened. "My *pai* lived on this farm for seventy years, and olive growing is the only life he knew. I am trying my best to honor his legacy."

"From what Veronica says, you take your work very seriously, to the point of excess."

"*Sim*, and with no apologies, I will continue to do so."

"Sometimes you need a break from all your demands."

"Not often."

She bristled. "Will you please, please, please take me to Medão Grande Beach? The trip would mean so much to me."

Hard-bitten inflexibility settled over Adolfo's face. His spiky black lashes lowered. He splashed more wine into his glass and didn't answer.

# CHAPTER 9

*A*dolfo stared out at the droplets of rain pattering against the double-hung windows of the guest cottage. Dark clouds rolled against a late afternoon sky. A half day of tree pruning lost, and he might lose another if the rain continued. Meanwhile, the bills steadily mounted.

"How do you celebrate Christmas in America?" he asked, forcing their conversation away from Krystal's request. "Any favorite memories?"

Her gaze narrowed. "Suppose you tell me why you want to know?"

"I'm interested."

She tore her glare from his and centered her attention on a water spot dampening the vaulted ceiling. "Why?"

"I don't know."

"What do you mean you don't know? You're the one who asked."

He raked a hand through his hair. "I haven't been certain of anything since the day I watched you on your surfboard. You were so calm, so well-balanced, so ... stunning. And my uncertainty grows stronger each time I'm around you."

"Should I be happy about that?"

"I'm certainly not."

She took her time and studied him. "And yet you continue to see me."

"Because I can't stay away." His gaze moved meaningfully to her full lips. It took all his restraint not to take her in his arms and kiss her.

Her cheeks pinkened. His admission hung in the ensuing silence.

He fidgeted and clasped his hands together. "I can't help worrying that the next time you're facing disaster; I won't be able to rescue you in time."

Memories surged. Memories of being helpless on Medão Beach while she'd nearly drowned. Senseless, that was what surfing was. No one could battle battering waves. His heartbeat had thrashed in his ears when he'd sped to the shore to help carry her to safety.

A hint of humor flickered in the corners of her eyes. "I'm flattered you're concerned. May I remind you that I can take care of myself?"

"Can you?"

His response was curt. He blamed the curtness on the previous month's labor-intensive harvest, combined with his angst and regret since his father's death. He'd been angry and irritable with everything. All these factors created chaos with his mood, reasoning and sentiments, especially when he sat a scarce few inches away from this captivating woman, her fragrance reminding him of freshness and the sea. Around her, his senses came alive.

"Will you at least consider taking me and the twins to the beach?" she asked.

"We can resume this discussion later in the week, after we learn the weather forecast. Sorry, it's the best I can offer."

She huffed an assent, apparently mollified. *At least for now.*

He braced his elbows on his knees. "Any more olive bread in your pantry?"

"Of course. I can't eat an entire loaf by myself."

"Do you want me to get a few slices for us?" He stood. "The bread has been on my mind."

*As well as the exquisite woman who'd baked it.*

"I'll go." She hurried to the kitchen, reappearing with a plateful of olive bread covered with creamy butter. "The bread is two days old," she reminded him, setting cloth napkins on the trunk.

He congratulated himself on successfully diverting her thoughts from surfing and helped himself to a slice of bread. "Tasty and a tad hard, the way I like it," he lied around a mouthful. He'd be chewing for hours.

"Thanks. I'm so glad." She arranged herself on the far end of the sofa. "I think I told you that I didn't have enough flour, so I substituted sugar."

"Ah, I can taste the extra sweetness." He planted a most charming smile on his face. "*Delicioso!*"

He was probably overdoing it.

"Are you lying?"

"I don't lie." Well, maybe now and then, when he didn't want to hurt someone. A white lie, a harmless untruth.

She arranged a napkin on her lap and picked up a corner piece of bread. "Will you share something about yourself?"

Was that a question? Yes, unfortunately. The conversation was supposed to be about her, not him.

He swallowed the bread, sat next to her on the sofa, and downed the port. "What would you like to know?"

Daintily, she chewed. "Anything, as long as you're honest."

"How about *dishonest?*"

She offered a curious look. "Sure. Go ahead."

He threw one arm carelessly across the back of the sofa.

"Earlier, I texted Veronica and she said you were alone in the cottage."

"You told me that."

"*Sim*. What I didn't say was that I bribed her. She was on her way here when I insisted I would check on you instead. We were both concerned."

"Another bribe like the poinsettia? What did you use this time?"

He withheld a laugh. "I volunteered to mind the twins. Believe me, a bigger sacrifice can't be found anywhere in all Europe."

"Should I be flattered? I suppose I should be. Does this mean you were worried about me?"

"Always."

She drew a shaky breath, her expression speculative.

"Now you," he prompted. "Favorite Christmas memories?"

"You didn't tell me any of yours."

He shrugged. "Someday, I will."

Actually, he'd prefer they make their own Christmas memories together, right here in Portugal.

She set her napkin on the trunk. "One Christmas, when I was five years old, my dad wanted my brother and me to send out Christmas cards. Dad asked me to lick the stamps and my brother sealed the envelopes. I treasured the thought that we were a real family, just like all the other families I knew from school."

The flickering candlelight accentuated her shimmering eyes. "I can still picture the front of that card—a big green wreath with a gigantic red bow. Inside the card was a glossy Christmas photo of my Dad, Julio, and me, all dressed up for Christmas. I wore a jade-green dress with a gold spangled headband, Julio wore a black vest, pants, and a red striped tie, and Dad wore a navy suit. On each card, Dad hand wrote, 'Merry Christmas from the Walters.'" She linked her fingers on her lap and gazed down at her hands. "So, that's my memory."

He imagined her, a motherless blonde and blue-eyed girl. Tenderness stirred in his chest. He wasn't a crier, but he still had to turn his head slightly so she wouldn't see him wipe the corner of his eye. Clearly, she missed having a mother.

"I love your story, I really do." Turning back to her, he slid his forefinger across her soft cheek.

She shrugged him off.

He pushed out a frustrated breath. "You did it again."

"Did what?"

He held up his hand and counted off three fingers. "You draw back every time I touch you."

"I haven't noticed."

"Sure you have. Care to tell me why?"

Her chin came up a notch. She was one stubborn American.

"If you explain, I'll take you to Peniche, as long as the weather cooperates."

"You're offering me a bargain?"

"*Sim.*"

"Unfair."

"On the contrary, my offer is beyond fair, considering my opinion on the subject of you and the beach."

She accorded him an uneasy smile. "Finally, I can surf?"

"I didn't say anything about surfing. I'll honor my bribe to Veronica." He skimmed Krystal's silky hair, pleased she didn't pull back. "Agreed?"

Her face reddened. "Do I have a choice?"

"The decision is up to you."

She pinched her bottom lip and studied the V neck of his sweater. "At least I'll get to play with the children and enjoy the ocean." When she finally connected with his gaze, she was like a magnet, all enticing charisma. Pulling him in, slowly, inexorably, her eyes a fathomless pool of wariness and want. Everything about her lightened his mood. She revived his flagging spirits—he'd been in such despair after his father's death. And he liked the feelings of revival, of lightness.

Women had accused him of being detached and aloof. Perhaps it was his nature, perhaps his upbringing. With Krystal, the urge to protect her from her foolish pursuits was so overpowering, he wanted to wrap his arms around her and never let go.

Unhurriedly, his fingers outlined the shape of her mouth, admiring the exquisite cupid's bow. He kept everything feathery—his caresses, his voice, his motions. Dressed in form-fitting jeans and a red blouse draped attractively around her enticing body, she was incredibly desirable.

His lips came within a fraction of hers. "What are you afraid of, Krystal?"

"Afraid is a strong word." In the course of shaking her head, she smiled, cancelling out both reactions. "Maybe you should explain why you feel so unbalanced around me, and why—"

"Why, why, why," he murmured. Her fragrance reminded him of crisp soap and clean water, a veil of sparkling simplicity. *Take it slow. Don't startle her.*

She was every inch the enchantress. She could be furious with him, and then disarm him the next moment with her charismatic smile.

Surely, she felt what he felt, this fate weaving a spell around them both.

She laid a finger on his jaw and drew a wobbly sigh. "Adolfo, I …I haven't been kissed in a long time."

He captured her sigh with a kiss. Their breaths mingled.

JOSIE RIVIERA

He claimed her quivering lips exhaustively, insistently, hungrily. Tentatively at first, her mouth answered his, surprising him with her eagerness.

His kiss deepened. His hands explored every inch of her flawless face, and he brought her tighter against him. Her exquisite body was made to fit against his.

When the kiss ended, she rested her head on his chest, her fingers flat against his shoulders.

He waited until their breathing slowed. Tenderly, he tilted her chin. "Please explain."

Her glorious eyes gleamed with disoriented tears. "Explain what?"

"Why you are so skittish."

"I don't know where to begin."

He pressed a kiss to her temple, content she allowed him to still hold her. "Start off wherever you're comfortable."

His answer seemed to amuse her.

She licked her lips, still lush and swollen from their kiss. "Do you know how old I am?"

Such an odd question. He chuckled against her fragrant hair, scents of leafy greens and musky soap. "According to Veronica, you'll soon be thirty years old."

"You're thirty-five. I asked Veronica about you too."

"And it cannot be disputed that Veronica is a wealth of information."

He was five years older than Krystal, and a million times more experienced. Work in the fields was grueling and back-breaking, while she was all softness.

She flicked him a glance. "Have you ever been married?"

"No. The perfect woman has eluded me."

*Until now.* The thought came unbidden, although he was already making plans for them—beginning with their excursion to Peniche, then intimate holiday dinners, a trip to

66

Lisbon to view the massive Christmas market, afterward taking in a classical concert at one of the local churches.

"Were you ever involved in a serious relationship?" he asked.

"Yes."

His heart rate increased, sending a flush through his body. He hadn't expected her response, at least not *that* response. He should have, though. It would be unusual for a thirty-year-old woman not to have had a serious relationship. But he doubted she was in one now. If she were dating someone, that man would have traveled to Portugal to support her at the surfing competition.

Still, he treaded carefully, picking up on her somber tone. "If you would rather not tell me ..."

When had she grown so distant? She visibly was withdrawing into herself, like a turtle retreating into its shell. She folded and unfolded the napkins, her movements slow and uncertain. "No. I need to talk about my past."

Her conflicted features said otherwise, reflecting his fears. One part of him wanted to know every detail of her life. The other part didn't want to hear what she obviously had avoided telling him up till now.

He couldn't summon the energy to stand, so he sat where he was, his arm around her shoulders.

"I should've told you," she began. "I thought Veronica might have said something." She rubbed the heel of her hand against her chest. "My husband, Ernie, died in a surfing accident three years ago. You see, I'm a widow."

Adolfo loosened his grip. He tried to ignore the shockwave of her statement, the impact her gorgeous, tear-streaked face had on his gut.

"I'm sorry for your loss." He attempted to keep his voice emotionless, knew he failed. "What was your husband like?"

"Ernie was popular with our peers, for one. I waitressed

while he devoted his days to chasing waves. Nothing worried him, and I soon learned his priorities were much different from mine. We were married only four months and I kept my maiden name, Walters." She refused to meet Adolfo's stare. "In retrospect, we were so young. Too young."

# CHAPTER 10

*L*ater that evening, Adolfo stomped up the marble porch stairs of his home and into the front room. He jerked off his jacket and flung it on a chair, followed by his boots skidding across the smooth pine floor. He flicked the light switch. No, in his mood, better to keep the lights off.

Krystal had been married to another man. His Krystal. His. Krystal.

She was a delightful blend of cool musk and satin skin and soft sobs.

He'd touched her as gently as his calloused hands allowed, kissed her so as not to frighten her. So many women welcomed his advances. With her, he waited for permission before a first caress, a tender kiss.

Never, never, never in his wildest imaginings had he supposed she was a widow.

He sank into his favorite armchair, gazing out the floor-to-ceiling windows at the moonlit mountain range beyond. The rich glow of an antique rosewood cabinet settled against an exposed brick masonry wall. His home blended the past with the present.

On the drive, his shock had faded. She was yielding to him and beginning to trust him. She'd allowed him to kiss her, touch her. Her mouth had answered his avidly. She was delightful, a combination of wholesome exuberance and fortitude, spirit and resolve.

He linked his hands behind his head and stared at the sweeping spiral staircase leading to his second-story bedroom.

He took joy in each minute of their time together. She forced him to work hard for her favor, and every smile was a triumph. When he considered their upcoming excursion to the beach, his pulse kicked up a notch.

Had she loved her husband? He assumed so, even if Krystal acknowledged that she and Ernie were too young when they married. Perhaps it was her girlish dream to marry the trendy guy in their tight-knit surfing community.

*Love.*

Love had no place in Adolfo's life. He welcomed bachelorhood, where life was regimented and made perfect sense. Finally, he was in control of the farm. Nevertheless, he had no control over his feelings for Krystal.

He leaned back against the leather armchair, recalling her twinkling gaze whenever she sparred with him. He shook his head. No use denying what was clear in his heart. He was already half in love with her.

Every movement she made, each time her cheeks flared with color when she laughed at one of his teasing remarks, his heart struck one unsteady beat after another.

To prevent being hurt again, she'd erected a tidy wall to keep men out of her life.

Understandable.

Nonetheless, he intended to breach those walls.

"Are the Portuguese trying to outdo the Americans?" she'd teased.

He'd prefer a tie. An American woman and a Portuguese man as equal partners.

Soon, he anticipated showing Krystal his home. Once it had been a deteriorating structure that no one wanted. He'd done much of the reconstruction himself, doing a full-scale mock-up beforehand, and was pleased with the results. He looked forward to Krystal's reaction.

With that final contemplation, he climbed the spiral staircase to his bedroom.

# CHAPTER 11

Krystal awoke to bright sunshine streaming through her bedroom window. It was the morning of their beach outing.

A few evenings earlier, it had been a relief to talk to Adolfo about Ernie, and she'd appreciated Adolfo's reserved sympathy. He didn't interrupt, he'd just listened. As a result, her sadness over Ernie's death had lessened.

She threw back the bedcovers and opened the window, inhaling the thick, fruity aroma of—what else—olives.

The distinctive quality of rich coffee and corn bread smeared with strawberry preserves made her lips smack. Adapting to the Portuguese continental breakfast certainly came easy.

She luxuriated in a long bath, washing herself with gardenia and vanilla-scented soap in the soaking tub, then arranged her hair in a ponytail. For want of a better style, she tucked her stubborn waves beneath a royal-blue baseball cap so that the ponytail stuck out the back of the cap. A black scalloped bikini, topped with a turquoise T-shirt, cut-off jeans shorts, and casual leather sandals completed her beach outfit.

With a sliver of optimism, she placed her wetsuit and surf gear in her bag. *Just in case.*

Adolfo had mentioned a visit to Peniche's city center for dinner, so she also packed a change of clothes. And, he said he'd planned a surprise for her.

As he pulled up to the cottage, the twins in the backseat of his truck, she glanced at the clock. He'd assured her that he'd arrive by eleven, and, once again, he proved a man of his word.

For the picnic, Krystal crowded a wicker basket with bottled water and *chourico*—a Portuguese smoked sausage. She included artisan cheese for the twins, and Adolfo had brought a loaf of Veronica's sweet bread.

"Did you bring pails and shovels?" she asked.

"*Sim.*"

"I'll get a spatula. It's for a sand sculpture," she explained at his questioning look.

He was about to close the lid of his trunk when Krystal reappeared on the porch holding her surfboard and gear.

He stared at her, the surfboard, then back at her. "No."

She tightened her fingers around the board. "I can't go to the beach without Angel."

He blinked. "Your surfboard's name is Angel?"

"Lots of surfers name their boards, and I believe in angels."

He studied his knuckles before meeting her jutting chin. "Today is for having a good time at the beach and a picnic lunch. Agreed?"

She opened her mouth and then closed it again as her arguments warred with reason. Granted, he was right. This day was earmarked for the children, not surfing. She set the surfboard in the cottage and descended the porch stairs to his truck.

After assisting her into the passenger seat, he asked if she'd experienced any dizziness lately.

"Headaches, mostly. Dizziness, once."

He slid into the driver's seat and turned the key in the ignition. "More justification why I can't allow you to surf. I'm too concerned about your safety."

"Overly concerned." Despite her disappointment, she managed to keep her tone reasonable.

"I'm practical. There's a difference."

Any room in her mind for retorts was quickly forgotten. The twins chattered incessantly, interspersing their periodic backseat squalls with giggles when Krystal attempted to sing "We Wish You a Merry Christmas" in Portuguese.

Adolfo squeezed her hand while he drove, his low-toned laugh ever present. "Your voice is lovely. Please keep singing."

"Uncle Adolfo, is Krystal your *namorada?*" Bernardo bellowed from the backseat.

"Only if she wants. She may still be angry at me."

"Why?"

"Because today she wanted to bring her surfboard named Angel, and I said no. And I'll tell you boys a secret. She doesn't need a surfboard. Krystal is already an angel, my angel from America."

His voice, so quiet, so affectionate, brought unbidden moisture to her eyes. She blinked and glanced at him. "Will agreeing to be your girlfriend earn me another Christmas log and more compliments?"

A smile spread across his face. "I have something better planned."

* * *

"UNCLE ADOLFO, did you pack our pails and shovels?" the ever-inquisitive Bernardo asked when they arrived at the beach. "Mom said Krystal knows how to make sand castles since she spent so many years at the shore."

"And," Krystal said, "I know how to build award-winning sand snowmen."

"Award-winning?"

"Well, not exactly, although the locals applauded the second I was finished. They were easy."

"The applauding locals were easy, or your sculptures?" Adolfo asked.

"Both. Sand snowmen don't take a lot of skill."

He tugged at her ponytail. "I like your hair pulled back, by the way. The style shows off your high cheekbones."

"Thanks." She felt her face heat from the sincerity in his gaze.

Laden with beach gear and the picnic lunch, they crested the dunes and found a grassy spot bordered by dense forest a few minutes later. Adolfo had avoided Medão Beach, Krystal noted, substituting it with an unspoiled strand several miles away.

Frothy whitecaps glistened in the afternoon sunshine. Krystal checked the surfing forecast app on her phone, confirming her observations that the swells were nonexistent. She glanced at the ocean and then quickly looked away. A vivid memory of nearly drowning flew through her mind.

She yanked off her baseball cap and threw it on the sand. Today wasn't a good day to surf, anyway.

Despite the twins' protests, she applied sunscreen to their slender, wiggling bodies, while Adolfo set towels and blankets adjacent to a large shade tree.

"My striped towel is lucky," she pointed out. "At least, it used to be."

"*Boa sorte*, good luck, is the order of the day." Adolfo patted the boys' tousled hair. "The water's too chilly for swimming. You can run along the shore."

"*Viva!*" The twins frolicked in the shallow waves, splashing each other, while Krystal and Adolfo watched, occasionally waving. They emerged from the water with chattering teeth and lips blue from the cold. Krystal toweled them off and then bundled them in thermal sweat suits.

She and Adolfo sailed a Frisbee through the air with the twins. When the boys tired of Frisbee throwing and opted to scramble like crabs, she sat beneath a tree. Adolfo came to sit beside her. He dusted his sandy hands on his khaki shorts and drained a bottle of water without taking a breath. Giving her a wicked smile, he reached into his pocket and produced a tree-shaped chocolate.

She drew nearer. "For me?"

He raised a forefinger to his lips. "For us. I don't want to ruin the boys' lunches."

An eye roll was in order. "How considerate of you."

With a furtive glance toward the twins, he unwrapped the chocolate. "We can split a piece each."

"Split? As in fifty-fifty, or ninety-ten?"

"Whatever is fair."

"Fifty-fifty."

He laughed, snapped the chocolate in half, and granted her a piece. "See how well we get along?"

She sampled the chocolate and then she stretched, cat-like, her smile expanding.

After lunch, the boys wrestled for a few minutes on the soft sand. Giggling rascally, they scampered farther away with each of Krystal's fruitless attempts to pull them apart.

"I told you to wear your running shoes," Adolfo reminded her.

"Watch this. They will come to me." She slipped off her shorts and shirt, donning a sheer black cover-up over her bikini. She nabbed two pails, shovels, and the kitchen spatula. Walking along the shore, she occasionally paused and dug down, then finally dropped the pails and knelt.

"I found a good spot," she announced. "Good quality sand makes all the difference."

"What are you building, Krystal? Let me see!" Bernardo shouldered his brother in his race to reach her first.

"Each of you gets a pail of water and three buckets of firm sand. Be sure the sand sticks together like this. And bear in mind, no rocks. The finer the sand, the better." She packed a handful of sand into a ball and rotated the ball in her hand. "Our snowman consists of three round balls of different heights arranged on top of each other."

The boys and Krystal occupied the next hour creating various-sized snowmen, shaping and smoothing, while Adolfo snapped photos of the trio with his cell phone.

"Uncle Adolfo, will you help us?" Bento asked.

Adolfo stretched out his legs. "I'm relaxing my sore muscles because pruning took a lot of effort this week. Besides, you don't need me. You're learning from an award-winning sand sculpture expert."

Krystal laughed. "Is there such a person?"

"Her name is Krystal." Beaming a white smile, he placed his hands behind his head and leaned against the bark of the tall shady pine.

Afterward, when the twins settled on their linen beach blankets for a nap, Krystal sat next to Adolfo.

He was outrageously attractive, his navy polo clinging to his wide shoulders, the top buttons casually undone. As the day progressed, the lines on his forehead had relaxed. His entire bearing seemed younger, as though time had rewound him to his youth. Laughing often as he'd tossed the Frisbee, he'd displayed a laidback side she hadn't seen before.

He pulled her close. A raw teasing of salt and sea air stung her lips, and a cool breeze glided over her skin. Nearby, orange trees popped with fruit, sunlight filtered through the shrubbery, the woods halcyon and serene. Sun versus shadows. In the approaching dusk, everything appeared calmer.

Adolfo partially closed his eyes.

With an outbreath of satisfaction, Krystal leaned nearer him, savoring the view of the dramatic Atlantic coastline. "I love this spot," she said.

Of course, she'd never see this strand of beach again. She'd been so determined to quit Portugal ... but how could she leave this fairy-tale country—and this gentle man holding her as if she were a piece of precious china?

As the sun set over the hills, she pressed her cheek against his chest and sighed. "We should go before it gets any later."

"Not until you eat this last morsel of chocolate." He fished in his pocket and displayed the tiniest piece of chocolate she'd ever seen. "I saved this for you."

"I wouldn't dream of denying you of your favorite pastime—eating every bit of chocolate in sight."

He laughed and popped the chocolate into her mouth. She savored the sweetness on her tongue.

His amusement was replaced by a lingering stare. "There is another pastime I like even better than eating chocolate."

Intensity in his eyes grew and her pulse tripled. She gloried in the excitement of his hard chest pressed against her, his lips moving lightly, then more urgently on hers. Straining to be nearer him, she kissed him back, winding her arms around his neck.

"Let's stay like this," he whispered. "Just like this."

Eyes closed, she listened to the rhythmic sound of the surf, the cawing of seabirds, the palm trees lightly swaying in the early evening breeze. The sheer splendor of it brought a quiet, wonderful peace.

"If only I weren't leaving," she murmured.

"You don't have to leave." His arms tightened around her. She opened her eyes to see his half smile, although the previous light-heartedness had faded from his expression.

# CHAPTER 12

*A*dolfo stopped smiling as Krystal withdrew from his grasp.

"You know my father needs me in Rhode Island."

"Do I?"

Her mutinous glare leveled on him. "If you've been listening to me these past two weeks, then you most certainly do."

She wouldn't like his next remark. He took a leap, anyway. "Your father is a grown man. Allow him to make his own decisions. Something tells me he would be happier in the senior facility where he could meet new friends."

"I know him. You don't."

"Fair enough." He rubbed his hands over his face. "We will agree to disagree, *sim*? No need to spoil a good day by quarreling."

She busied herself with shaking out towels, pulling on her cut-offs, T-shirt, and a pink terry-cloth jacket. No matter what she wore, she was gorgeous. It was difficult, but he turned away.

Their discomfort ended when Bento opened his eyes

from his nap. "I'm hungry!" His loud proclamation quickly awoke his sleeping brother.

"We'll stop for pizza," Adolfo said.

Thirty minutes later, they were window-shopping at the little seaside shops situated on Peniche's boardwalk. Afterward, sitting astride a stone wall overlooking the sea, they waited for their pepperoni pizza to cool and ate outside. A pastry shop located next door to the pizzeria sold *bolo rei*, king cake, an agreeably sweet Christmas cake, along with beautifully-crafted marzipan.

Krystal declared she'd eat dessert first, casting a wary eye on Adolfo and refusing to go halves with him.

He grinned. "In the past, king cake contained a broad bean, which hid a good luck charm. Granted, the tradition is no longer observed due to safety precautions. But the person who got the slice with the bean provided the cake the following year."

"So, no bean is inside, and therefore, no luck?" She plucked the crystallised fruit off the top and handed it to him.

He happily accepted. "On the contrary, you're in Portugal during the Christmas season. How lucky can you get?"

Dusk swiftly cooled the coastal air. Krystal tugged thick hooded sweatshirts over Bento and Bernardo before they dashed off to troll for seashells and colored glass.

Adolfo grasped her hand. "In your bungalow, did you invest in a real or artificial Christmas tree?"

"Artificial. Certainly, I prefer a real tree." She drew an unsteady breath. "For the past three years, there hasn't been a Christmas tree in my house."

"For the sake of honoring your late husband?"

"Yes. The memories were too difficult." Sadness shadowed her eyes. "We married on a whim, and I soon understood I'd wedded a lifestyle choice."

"Whose lifestyle choice?"

"In all fairness, both of ours. We were happy-go-lucky surfers—despite the fact I earned the actual income. Still, we struggled to meet our monthly rent payments." She shook her head. "Fortunately, I surfed in a lot of events and banked some winnings, which was how I afforded my bungalow."

And during that time, she'd evidently dismissed the countless concussions.

Adolfo considered her in thoughtful silence. Even if he disagreed with every aspect of her perilous sport, he was humbled by her dauntless resolve to succeed.

"The minute I traveled to Portugal for the competition, I vowed I'd never live in the past again." She squared her shoulders. "I'm ready to embrace life."

"You are one plucky woman," he said, his lips a hairs-breadth from hers. With his hands, he framed her face and entangled her spirited affirmation with a lengthy kiss.

The high color of her face, her magnificent eyes a bottomless indigo, dragged him deeper. Each time she allowed him to hold her, his blood raced like fire through his veins.

# CHAPTER 13

*A* couple hours later, Adolfo swung into the U-shaped driveway of Veronica and Clemente's traditional country house. He had insisted on dropping the twins off before going on to Krystal's cottage, and she waited in his truck.

The boys tracked sand through the foyer as Adolfo propelled them into the kitchen. They struggled to one up each other, talking louder, one over the other, so that their parents were bombarded with two editions of the same beach adventure.

Offering a quick wave to Clemente and a quicker explanation to Veronica, Adolfo assured them that the boys would sleep well that night. "Besides tearing about all day, they sang constantly during the ride home."

Veronica beamed. "They sing like cherubs. They always remind me of the Vienna Boys choir."

Not quite, Adolfo thought, although he nodded.

"Did they sleep in the car?" Clemente asked.

"Never. They switched from one Christmas carol to

another, singing again and again and again." *And again. How many verses of "Jingle Bells" were there?*

Veronica finger-combed the boys' tangled hair. "Thanks for allowing them to join you for such a fun day."

"My pleasure." And, Adolfo realized with a start, that he meant it.

A few minutes later, he and Krystal reached the cottage. He cut the engine and placed a kiss on her cheek. "Ready for your surprise?"

She grinned. "I love surprises."

A slight gust flapped the hem of her pink jacket as he assisted her from his truck. The evening's fog slowed their footsteps.

"What's this?" Her eyes widened at the sight of a large pine tree on the porch.

"Your surprise. I arranged for it to be delivered while we were at the beach. No Portuguese home is complete without a Christmas tree."

They ran up the steps, the vivid evergreen scent permeating the night air.

"Do you like it?" He glanced at her, unsure of her reaction.

Tears welled in her eyes. "I love it. Thank you!"

He bowed his head and uttered a thankful prayer. Apprehension had chattered in his brain all the way to the cottage. He'd envisioned himself hauling the tree back to his truck under Krystal's furious stare.

He let out a huge breath and dragged the tree into the cottage.

After he'd deposited the tree in a corner, he wrapped his arms around her. "I'll buy bells and pinecone chocolates tomorrow. We can string and hang them on the tree tomorrow night."

"Adolfo, I can't wait!" Her laughter lit the room. "When I

was a little girl, I loved fat colored lights and silver tinsel on our tree."

He bit his lower lip to keep from smiling. "We'll trim your Portuguese tree with lights and tinsel and chocolate."

"And I'll prepare dinner."

"Really? You cook?"

She cocked her head, feigning offense. "I like cooking. I'm not a gourmet chef by any means. I'm better at baking."

He decided not to touch that comment and made a vague compliment about her exceptionally sweet and succulent olive bread.

They exchanged grins overflowing with contentment. And something else. Companionship. Kindred spirits, both searching for acceptance and love.

Krystal wedged herself into a corner of the sofa. A cool breeze kicked through the open living room window, blowing blonde strands around her face. She tucked a strand behind her ear and smiled at him.

He smiled back. There was an ethereal quality about her that captivated him, a slow burn rather than a sudden hit. But it was there. *Sim*, it was there. Their relationship had developed quicker than he'd ever imagined, and he was powerless to stop the attraction.

He drew a lungful of air and slowly let it out. The contented expression on her face mirrored his feelings. He pressed a kiss on her temple, then built a fire in the hearth.

"How do you harvest olives?" she asked.

He sat beside her. "Do you like to climb trees?"

"What does climbing trees have to do with harvesting olives?" She playfully shoved at his chest. "Julio and I once built a tree house in our backyard and climbed that tree a dozen times a day. Does that count?"

Adolfo sighed dramatically. "Where were you last month?

I needed you desperately when olive harvest season rolled around and we were short extra hands."

He needed her desperately now, although he didn't add that part.

He chucked her chin. "Harvesting is beyond time-consuming, and it takes three people several hours to harvest two trees."

"How is it done?"

"You can either climb a ladder, or climb the tree. I prefer to use an olive rake and smack the stick on the tree."

"Sounds exhausting."

"*Sim,* though when I'm outside on a wintry day, the sun on my face, appreciating the views of the hillside and every color of the rainbow ... Well, these moments make a hard task incredibly rewarding."

"So rewarding you'll be adding grape vines to your workload?"

"Olives and grapes share similar processing, because each is pressed and put up. When wine-press work ends, olive pressing begins." He paused. "Do you think a winery is feasible?"

He didn't usually ask for other people's opinions, except for Clemente. However, here beside him sat his splendid, exquisite Krystal, and he valued her insight.

Pensive silence stilled the space for several seconds.

"Yes, it's an excellent idea," she said. "If I stayed, I'd help you plant the vines and start your winery."

She could. Stay. He left the thought alone, pulling in a sigh thick with the utter loneliness he'd feel in her absence. "Clemente approves, and he's the guy who writes the checks. Remember, the winery business is fierce and our family could end up losing money."

He spoke as if she were already part of the Silva family. Had she noticed?

For a moment, her body went rigid.

She'd noticed.

"Knowing you and your work ethic," she said, "your wine will taste better than any competitor." Her encouraging smile made his heart race. He wanted to hold her, to feel her small hand brushing against his chest. He wanted her to be attracted to him, an olive farmer with no formal education.

Sometimes, his sadness at his father's death, his frustration to produce a profitable farm, was like a needle jabbing at his skin. Sometimes, he thought about walking away from it all. He knew that would never happen, his obligation to his heritage long entrenched. And he felt safe there, amidst the vast acreage.

"I appreciate your confidence." He spread his knees and studied the hardwood floor between his sandals. "As I told you, years ago I suggested planting grapes to my father. I supposed he'd pat me on the back and congratulate me. On the contrary, he shot my idea down and insisted we stick with the old ways, the old traditions."

"Perhaps your father was a tad stubborn. Perhaps you resemble him more than you realize."

There was substance in her remark. "Perhaps." Besides, his agreement brought a perfect excuse to gather her in his arms and kiss her. She was a woman who needed to be kissed, he decided, thoroughly and often.

Once the kiss ended, they remained in companionable silence and stared at the fire kindling in the grate.

He brushed his lips against her temple. "What are you thinking?"

"When I first came to Portugal, I didn't want to like this country. And I definitely didn't want to like you."

He laughed. "I felt the same about you."

She drew back and studied him. "And now?"

"Now things are different. Do you agree?"

"Yes, very different." Her cornflower-blue eyes softened with affection. She brushed a hand back and forth across his cheek. "You don't need to take care of me anymore. You've had enough of that."

"I didn't mind."

"And I'm sorry you've lost so much work time because of me."

"So am I."

Her fingers halted. "I said I'm sorry."

"You're forgiven." Nuzzling her neck, he chuckled. "I've hired someone to help me so I'll have more free time."

*To spend with her.*

She tilted her head. "Who?"

"Francisco. He starts tomorrow."

He could almost see the questions pushing into her busy brain. "You said you wouldn't hire him because he's unreliable."

Adolfo's smile had no penitence. "I changed my mind. I thought about your brother's story, and you're right. Everyone, even Francisco, deserves a second chance."

Indisputably, prison had changed Francisco. For better or for worse, time would tell.

# CHAPTER 14

*T*hree more days gone. Krystal used the time to develop a business plan for her still-unnamed swimwear company, perusing specialized artists' and manufacturers' websites. If only her sketches were more expert. She could envision the swimsuits, but hadn't managed to convey the ideas to paper.

Despite that frustration, she was anticipating another amazing evening with Adolfo. The hours with him brought a contentment she could scarcely explain.

After work, he stopped by his home to shower and then was knocking on her cottage door an hour later, laden with unique Christmas trimmings—a festive wreath, a tiled keepsake ornament, a campfire-plaid tablecloth. Always, he presented her with a jewel-toned bouquet complemented by greenery from the ever-abundant gardens surrounding the countryside.

She'd thank him and bury her nose in the sweet fragrance. And then he'd kiss her.

He brought ingredients for dinner, seafood being the norm. He proved to be an excellent cook, attesting to his years of living alone; and he taught her how to season cod with olive oil and vinegar, to prepare a simple clam stew, and to grill mouth-watering sardines. His homemade *piri piri*, a spicy hot sauce, usually accompanied the meals, as did a field-greens salad tossed in an oil and vinegar dressing.

She marveled at how a strong-shouldered, formidable man like him could move so capably around the kitchen. His tanned, muscled arms revealed by the short sleeves of his white cotton T-shirt, he attended to last-minute dinner preparations—setting the table, placing a single purple bud in a vase, summoning her to the table with another exquisite, lengthy kiss.

"Your cooking is so good," she told him after she'd tried a grilled sardine. Did she dare to dip it in the hot *piri piri* sauce?

He'd quirked a thick, dark eyebrow. "I also can iron and sweep a floor and wash windows fairly well when asked nicely."

He was generous, reliable, and a romantic. Whenever her glance lingered on his handsome face, he'd flash a teasing smile, and her pulse skipped a beat.

When dawn broke the following day, Krystal rushed to the kitchen. The surf finals were imminent, and she needed to practice. Her phone app stated the swells were ideal. Today was the day.

She called her cousin, setting her cell phone on speaker as she peeked out the window at another steamy December day.

"Can you please take me to Peniche, Veronica?" she asked. "If I want to improve, I have to get back in the water. You're pushing me against the wall."

On cue, Krystal's wrist burned. *That pain—it wasn't real. Her wrist had healed.*

While she spoke with Veronica, Krystal peered at the recipe for rice pudding—that Veronica had given her. Adolfo had offhandedly mentioned that rice pudding was a traditional Portuguese Christmas dessert and one of his favorites. Krystal glanced at the kitchen wall clock and calculated the hours to Peniche and back. He had already accepted her invitation for a formal dinner, and she planned to surprise him.

Veronica expounded on the dozen and one reasons why she wouldn't be available for Krystal, while Krystal measured rice and water and brought the pudding ingredients to a boil on the stove. Had she added enough brown sugar? She flooded the mixture with sugar, then gave the mixture a stir.

With a thin 'good-bye' to Veronica, Krystal disconnected the call. She began to suspect Veronica and Adolfo were in silent agreement, both deciding surfing was too risky a sport for Krystal to pursue.

Her stomach hardened as she replayed the conversation with Veronica.

*Why don't they listen to me? I told them I'm fine.*

A trace of pine scent, bringing childhood remembrances of Sunday morning waffles drenched in maple syrup, wafted through the cottage. Krystal drained the rice in a colander, ladled out a bowlful, and stepped into the living room. Pausing between spoonfuls, she delighted in the tree, decked with numerous chocolate Yuletide shapes. Pieces of oak burned in the hearth, the scent toasty and Christmassy. She hummed the first two measures of "We Wish You a Merry Christmas" and closed her eyes.

The previous night, she and Adolfo had trimmed the tree and set up a crèche to represent the Nativity. On Christmas Eve, many Portuguese families gathered around their crèches before attending church at midnight.

After his explanation, he'd traced her cheekbones with his thumbs, and gazed at her with unbearable gentleness.

"Please stay in Portugal for Christmas. I promise our time together will be magical. In January, we can travel to the

States and, hand in hand, we will make it up to your father. He'll understand why you postponed your return."

Gaze downcast, she stared at her hands.

"Will you at least consider my suggestion?"

His question held a guarded hope, and tears sprang to her eyes.

The subject of surfing was never mentioned. Apparently, he considered it no longer an issue.

But she did.

So she'd forced her lips together and lifted her gaze, studying his attentive face, resisting the temptation to fling herself into his capable arms and agree with his request. *Yes, yes, yes.*

Somehow, she'd managed not to respond at all.

Krystal shook away the thoughts, seated herself on the living room sofa and set down the bowl. Worn-out—by unfinished dreams, indecision, her inability to be a worthy daughter, her feelings for Adolfo—she splayed her fingers over her eyes and sobbed. Didn't Adolfo realize all those years she'd practiced to become one of the top seventeen women surfers in the world, and that all that work and sacrifice could culminate in winning the finals? Didn't he realize she couldn't disappoint her father?

Her mind spun. She couldn't let her scary wipeout damage her image of herself. The definition of Krystal Walters was strong, not weak.

Admit defeat? Never. She was an accomplished woman pursuing an up-and-coming career.

Numbly, she wandered to the bedroom and glided her fingers along the flat, familiar surface of her surfboard. "I'm trying, Angel. Adolfo told me that whatever challenge he faced, he intended to win. Well, he's met his match, because I mean to succeed too."

She carried the board into the living room, intending to

wax it.

A knock on the cottage door made her pause. Perhaps Adolfo had finished early.

Despite their last discussion, she was always happy to see him. Summoning a smile, she swung open the door.

Francisco lounged against the door frame, aviator glasses clipped to his button-down linen shirt. "*Bom dia*, my lovely *senhorita.*" He kissed her hand.

Her smile faded, and she jerked her hand back. "What are you doing here?"

"Were you expecting someone else?" His thin lips twitched with laughter. "Don't tell the boss I'm taking a respite from the hot sun. For over an hour, I've pruned his precious olive trees, while he hightailed it off to price grape vines."

"How did you know where I lived?"

Francisco jerked a shrug. "Common knowledge in a town like Évora. You're a fine-looking American woman who's also a world-renowned surfer." With a hawkish peer, he assessed the interior of the cottage. "Will you invite me inside for a drink?"

Coolly, she nodded and allowed him entry. He didn't give her much choice. Besides, he was Adolfo's friend.

Francisco made a show of complimenting the Christmas decorations. "Very cozy," he remarked in a sarcastic tone, sprawling in the armchair Adolfo frequented.

Krystal disappeared into the kitchen. "Is water all right?"

"For what?"

"You said you wanted a drink. I supposed you were thirsty."

"Anything stronger than water?"

For an overlong moment, she stared at the empty glasses in the cupboard. "Adolfo drinks port wine in the evening."

"I drink whiskey in the morning."

"Well, port is all I have."

He smirked. "Port it is."

Doubling back, she handed him the glass of wine.

"Do you always keep your surfboard in the living room?" he asked.

His gray-eyed appraisal unnerved her.

"I planned to wax my board. I anticipated practicing my surf maneuvers before the finals."

"What day are the finals?"

"Friday, and I haven't surfed since my wipeout. Today, I wanted to get to Medão Grande Beach. As usual, no one can take me."

Francisco took a liberal slug of port. "I can."

"Aren't you working?"

"I arrange my own hours. I'll ring Veronica once we're there and she can tell Adolfo. He'll understand. The shore beckons for a *belissimo senhorita*."

Krystal ran a hand through her hair. "Adolfo's one hundred and ten percent against me surfing. I had a concussion during the preliminary competition. Several concussions through the years, actually."

Francisco stood and closed the gap separating them. "Is that why you've been crying?"

Most people required at least three feet of personal space, and Francisco obviously hadn't gotten that memo. She took a step back.

"I miss being in the water. Surfing is my job, although it's more the thrill of nailing the ideal wave …" She shook her head. "Don't misunderstand, I appreciate why Adolfo feels the need to protect me."

"Hours tick by while you sit isolated in this cottage, waiting for him to decide if he should or shouldn't take you to Peniche. He wants total control over every situation, and never liked to share his women."

"I'm not his woman."

"Aren't you?"

"He's concerned about my health."

Francisco choked back a laugh. "You're defending him?"

"Yes, I suppose I am."

"Typical Adolfo. He charms the ladies and keeps the best for himself. He has dangled around you ever since you arrived." Francisco used the right amount of scorn, tempered by flattery.

She rocked on her heels and stared at the floor. "In fairness, I don't understand myself anymore. I want to surf, and then I don't."

"Therefore, I will decide for you. Let's go to the beach."

"I should finish the pudding preparations first. Adolfo said he loves—"

"Adolfo has a lot of loves, and the olive farm will always be his first. Meanwhile, Medão awaits your triumphant return."

She deliberated, shivering from an imaginary blast of Adolfo's icy gaze if he found out. *When* he found out. "You mean now?"

"Not everyone abides by rigid rules, unless you fancy a boring life. You're a surfer girl—you like being exposed to danger. Or are you afraid to ride your surfboard again after the wipeout?"

She wasn't afraid of surfing. She just wasn't certain she could muster the courage to face Adolfo's disappointment.

Her gaze darted to the kitchen. "We might be gone too long, and I promised—"

"Adolfo will be late getting back tonight."

"Did you know that this year we'll sell olives in the retail store? And in a few years, with the purchase of grape vines ..." She tried to piece disjointed ideas together. Had she said *we*?

Francisco subjected her to a long appraisal. His expression was so blasé, her self-control slipped a notch. "Are you aware his plans in Évora include meeting a woman for lunch? Since you're here by yourself, I assume he's seeing the stunning Isabel."

Her astonishment of Adolfo's betrayal stalled Krystal's breath, cut through her thoughts.

Sure, she didn't feel duty-bound to honor his request not to surf, though he hadn't asked, simply stated *no* in that flat, dismissive way of his.

"Isabel is the woman who won the beauty pageant several years ago?"

"*Sim.*"

Intending to gorge on carbohydrates and uncertainty, she sank onto the sofa and retrieved her half-eaten bowl of rice. "Adolfo didn't say a word about meeting anyone."

Francisco's smile never wavered. "It appears I'm the sole person around here who wants to help you."

She ran through her objectives.

Win. *Must* win.

Her wrist burned, and an unexpected headache struck with a vengeance.

*Live your life boldly and with temerity,* her father had encouraged.

"I'll be ready in five minutes." Like the determined athlete she was, she trooped to the bedroom and changed into her swimsuit, then snatched her wetsuit and surf equipment.

She peered into the kitchen. So much for finishing the rice pudding preparations.

Francisco clinked her bowl into the sink, singing "Jingle Bells."

In English.

He would be a nice rest from the intense Adolfo.

# CHAPTER 15

*a*fter learning about Adolfo's luncheon date, Krystal felt more like a deflated balloon than a world-class surfer. In the cottage's bathroom, she splashed cold water on her face and stared in the mirror. Her cheeks and lips were so thin. Was that a gray root peeking out from her blonde hair?

She stepped into the kitchen. Francisco had raided the cupboards and packed a jar of olives, a loaf of corn bread, bottled water, and the unfinished bottle of port for the drive to the beach.

When they left the cottage fifteen minutes later, her mood had lightened. Francisco's car, a sleek convertible, washed a bright red in the sunlight. Just as they buckled their seat belts, he disclosed, rather vaguely, that he'd borrowed the convertible from a friend.

*Oh no, I hope I'm not making the biggest mistake of my life.*

She slid into the passenger seat. Regardless of Francisco's easy-going manner, she wasn't certain his remark about Adolfo and Isabel rang true. The disbelief niggled, a reminder that despite whatever Adolfo might be doing in Évora, he had spent every evening with Krystal.

Perhaps the acres and acres of scarlet and bright yellow fields heard her reflections, because the trees rustled and sighed. She imagined the murmurings of secrets and dreams, ancient as the country of Portugal itself.

Francisco bore down on the accelerator. The car responded, careening along the narrow roadways. "Adolfo and I used to play in these streets, shoot at cans with rocks, drink foamy cups of cold beer on hot summer nights." He focused on her while he swerved around corners scarcely wide enough for one car and a skinny pedestrian.

"Typical males," she responded.

"What did Adolfo tell you about me?"

"You work in finance," she answered evasively.

"*Sim.* I rose to vice president of a manufacturing company before I was caught embezzling funds. My penchant is money, so finance proved a natural choice for my university studies."

And stealing, although she didn't add that.

"Adolfo didn't attend university," she said. Yet, a sharp intellect shone in his eyes.

"When we attended primary school, Adolfo never mentioned becoming a farmer. He planned to apply to a prestigious university in America," Francisco said. "Architecture interested him, and he was brilliant in math, analyzing and solving problems in half the time it took the rest of the class. But even though he graduated at the top of our class, he never quite fit in."

"Why didn't he go to college?"

"Probably because he was too busy thinking about olives." Francisco laughed. "His father needed him, and Adolfo's motto is obligation above all else."

Francisco kept reminiscing, and to avoid his endless prattle, Krystal feigned sleep. When he finally got the message and the conversation quieted, her thoughts shifted to Adolfo.

He was a handsome enigma, valuing his privacy and his ability not to rely on anyone.

She'd grown up without a mother, the odd person out, her solitary path. In an attempt to prove herself, she'd filled the void with surfing. Ernie came along, all sea-salty pizzazz, a guy who embodied the surf culture of perpetual youth, popularity and year-round summers.

Skinny, always shirtless, happy-go-lucky Ernie. The man she'd loved.

Right?

She frowned, repeating the question to herself.

Her mind raced, searching for answers.

Well, so she'd thought. Except when a swell brewed, Ernie could disappear for hours. Responsibility was a fleeting consideration on the fringe of his mind, and that was why he couldn't hold a job. Ernie was the exact opposite of Adolfo.

Adolfo's name brought a quiver to her chest. He paid attention to her, his hazel gaze unflinching. With him, she felt protected and secure. He was self-sacrificing and self-sufficient. Plus, his sense of humor was wonderful.

And those were merely some of the reasons why she was falling in love with him.

Her eyes flew open. What? No, no, no. She hadn't known him long enough to love him.

Or had she? She recognized that emotion flooding her heart. Without knowing it, he'd broken through her boundaries.

"I'll shield you from Adolfo's fury," Francisco was saying. "His temper can be fierce."

"I've never seen his temper. And please don't say anything bad about him."

*She was in love with Adolfo, a Portuguese farmer. A loner. A kind and generous man. A brilliant man. A man she innately knew would guard her with his life.*

She loved him with a solicitousness that made her fiercely protective of him, and a desperation that left her vulnerable and breakable.

He had a clear mind for business, foreseeably why his *pai* had chosen him, not Clemente, to assume the farm tasks. A sense of honor propelled him to accept his responsibilities. To please his father, he'd set aside his personal aspirations.

Francisco gestured to a patch of strawberry runners tangled over wooden fences, pasture dotted with sheep. "Not for me, this hard, thankless labor. I want people to look up to me."

Adolfo had taken up his father's olive rake rather than studying at his dream university. Meanwhile, Francisco had landed in prison. Thus the difference between honor and dishonor. People worked the edges. Some minded the guardrails, others didn't care. Adolfo was a man of integrity.

Francisco angled to face her. "Once he reached his teens, Adolfo wasn't permitted to have a good time. I never heard laughter coming from his house, probably why he snuck out with me and my friends." He waited a beat. "Did he ever tell you about his shouting matches with his father?"

"Their relationship was rocky."

"There's an understatement." Francisco's smile was quick. "More like two stubborn people who never gave in—father and son."

With a nod, she closed her eyes again and courted sleep. For the first time since getting into Francisco's car, she agreed with him.

# CHAPTER 16

*H*ours later, Krystal awoke when Francisco's convertible came to a stop and the bitter scent of raw ocean reached her nostrils. She hauled her surf gear out of the car and traipsed over broken driftwood and sandbanks to Medão Grande Beach. Francisco trailed beside her.

"Since all the locals think the water is too cold in December," he said, "the strand is yours. I prefer this cooler weather. In the summer, the temperature can exceed one hundred degrees Fahrenheit." Francisco peeled off his shirt, exposing a full-sleeve tattoo of an attractive woman with a spill of long black hair.

"A woman I love," he provided, at Krystal's quizzical stare. "Adolfo and I both got tattoos the day we graduated from secondary school."

"Is she the particular lady you mentioned when Adolfo and I met you in Évora?"

"*Sim.* When we attended secondary school, she didn't hide the fact that she preferred Adolfo, although he wasn't interested. Still, I continued to pursue her. She at least was my friend, but once I was arrested, she wanted nothing more to do with me."

"What is her name?"

"Isabel."

Krystal stiffened. "As in Isabel, the beauty queen?"

"*Sim.*"

"So Adolfo's tattoo is of Isabel, also?" Krystal turned away, intending to shake out her towel and place her surf gear on top. Her arms and legs refused to move, though.

"No, *senhorita.* His tattoo is inked on his back and is one unique word. *Saudade.*"

"What does *saudade* mean?"

"It is difficult to translate. Think of an occasion or person you keep forever in your heart and would miss if they were gone." Francisco positioned his emerald-green jacket on the sand and sat on it. "After secondary school graduation, he was undecided about his future. While the majority of our class planned to go on to university, he knew his formal schooling had ended. His father was slowing down and Clemente had been hired to work at a law office in town." Francisco popped open the olive jar and mopped up the juice with a slice of bread. With the bottle of port beside him, he sloshed himself a glass. "*Saudade* is joy and sorrow mixed together."

She waxed her surfboard in silence. *Joy and sorrow. Two different spectrums. Perhaps life could be found somewhere in the middle. Compromises. A new mindset.*

Atlantic breakers roared against a backdrop of sandstone cliffs. More and more, the same thought resonated in Krystal's mind: she'd miss Portugal, the fervor of the jubilant festivals, the jaw-dropping scenery that rendered her speechless.

And Adolfo. Adolfo most of all.

A dull ache settled in her chest when she pondered never seeing him again. How could she carry on if they were separated?

Francisco donned his aviators. "Aren't you jumping in the water?"

She glanced at the ocean, then away. The strong desire to surf whenever she was within walking distance of the sea eluded her. Did she *want* to surf anymore? She could scarcely look at the ocean without remembering how the enormous waves had tumbled her, tossed her, nearly drowned her.

"First, I'll take a walk to warm up." She hung a right, carving sandy footprints along the shore, avoiding tangled seaweed as she splashed through rocky pools, shallow and overrun with seawater.

She had gone behind Adolfo's back, and he would be furious. She knew him well enough to know that. Guilt overwhelmed her, because he credited her with being as honorable as him, and she'd betrayed his trust. Nonetheless, in his high-handed way, he limited her. And he was arrogant and exacting.

She shrugged the thoughts aside because he was also thoughtful and considerate. In her mind, she heard his roguish chuckle when he'd offered her the tree-shaped chocolate at the beach.

*I saved this for you.*

They shared so much more than chocolate—laughter, memories of their fathers, Christmas tree-trimming, and a stroll through his charming, historic town. There was no point in denying how much she cared for him just to keep her surfing goals alive. Even now, she longed for his lazy smile, approving glance, and the sound of his deep voice.

Sighing, she scuffed at a glossy-pink seashell with the toe of her sandal.

She'd appease Adolfo's anger by telling him what he wanted to hear, for she'd decided to remain in Portugal and spend Christmas with him.

When had she made that decision? That morning, last night, last week? Somehow, she'd known since she'd confessed to him that she hadn't wanted to like him. But she did. With a smile, he'd admitted the same.

She'd tell him tonight at the cottage. She envisioned his affable grin, the quiet hope in his eyes changing to gladness. A good man like him would never abandon her, knowing she'd given up so much to be with him. Assuredly, her caring father would understand.

Satisfied with her choice, she paced back and forth along the shore and planned their upcoming evening. First, she'd pin her hair in a casual upsweep away from her face, the way Adolfo liked it, and dress specially to please him. She'd brought a stunning satin sheath dress to Portugal in case of a formal occasion. It was embellished with lace sleeves, classic and elegant.

In her enticing outfit, Krystal would serve him her home-made rice pudding, and then, in that bold, sensual way of his, he'd compliment her on a tempting meal, take her in his arms, and kiss her.

Long, hard, and lingering.

Her heart galloped just at the thought of the kiss.

Yes, her life was finally in balance, and she was in love with a noble, unselfish man.

She walked back to Francisco.

"Ready to show me how well you navigate those waves?" he asked, slightly slurring his words.

She frowned. He wanted a performance? She'd give him one.

She pulled on her wetsuit and adjusted her reef socks and booties.

Fat, gray clouds had assembled in the sky, underscoring her need for haste. The swells were ideal, although conditions could suddenly change, dependent on the weather.

She secured the leash to her surfboard and paddled out, soon catching and riding a wave. *She could do this. The sudden stinging pain in her wrist? Only her imagination.*

The cool water refreshed, and the familiar rush of gliding up and down the waves invigorated. Her first maneuver, the frontside turn, required placing her weight on her back foot and bending her back knee. With ease, she leaned in the direction of the swell and reverted to the center.

She could see Francisco hold up his glass and toast her. Surely he hadn't been drinking all the while.

She pointed her attention to her next maneuver. Her backside turn was a little more complicated. To see the wave, she needed to peer over her shoulder, and she transferred her weight as she reached the top of the swell.

*Stay aligned and balanced.*

She tugged at the sleeves of her wetsuit, willing her muscles to relax. Normally, this maneuver came easily. Not today. Today, she felt lightheaded. Her body was overheating in the wetsuit. Her breath came short and fast.

*Ignore the wrist pain. It isn't real. You're very different from the child who huddled in a closet with a flashlight.*

She knew the moment she'd successfully accomplished the maneuver. Thrusting a fist toward the clouds, she let out an elated "Hurray!" Her gaze skirted the shore for Francisco's upraised glass.

Now where had he wandered off? Apparently, he couldn't sit still.

She kept scanning—

Her breath came to a halt.

Francisco stood at the water's edge with another man. A

tall, handsome man. The man's arms made sweeping gestures at Francisco before he swerved jerkily toward her.

Adolfo. Before she could avoid eye contact, his hard, flinty stare cemented on hers.

# CHAPTER 17

*I*t couldn't be Adolfo. He was buying grape vines in Évora, eating lunch and sipping espresso with the beauty queen.

The air became thin, sparking of disaster. Krystal couldn't breathe.

With a tumble off her surfboard, she wiped out into the frigid Atlantic waters.

"Krystal!"

She heard Adolfo's unnerved shout, saw his frenetic dash toward her. Hadn't he said he couldn't swim?

She regained her strength and paddled to shore. The brisk breeze cooled her heated face as she surfaced and unleashed her foot from the surfboard.

Slowly, she inhaled, intending to pick up her pace and hurry past him.

Adolfo seized her forearm. "What were you trying to prove out there?"

She noted the betraying hoarseness in his tone, the fear in his hazel eyes.

Her arms fell limply to her sides. She couldn't bear to see him upset.

"Don't worry. Please don't worry. I'm a pro in the water."

He held her firm. "Were you planning to walk right past me with no explanation?"

She yanked from his grasp and attempted to get by him. "Let go of me! Who do you think you are?"

His one-step twist blocked her path. "By your own admission, I'm the man who came to your rescue not once, but twice. Were you trying for a third time?"

She pressed back her hair, knowing it was a soaked, tangled mess. "You broke my concentration!"

"Suppose you got dizzy on those heavy waves? Then what? Dr. Dantas advised giving your brain time to heal."

"I'm so tired of you parroting the doctor's advice." She knew her face telegraphed her guilt. Who was she to pretend to know more than the doctor?

"No one fights the ocean and wins. Admit your limitations." Adolfo's voice grew softer. "Please, Krystal."

Through a blur of tears, she spun toward the parking area. He was in no state to listen to reason. "You're the one trying to limit me! You ruined my practice and I was doing well. I can't surf with you standing on shore glaring at me."

"I'm standing ready to save you."

"How? You can't swim." She shivered. The sun felt stiff and bleak against her wet skin. "I'm going back to the cottage. Francisco will take me."

Adolfo looked tired. And livid, his hazel eyes glittering a dangerous green. "You're coming with me."

"You're joking, right?"

Adolfo frowned at Francisco. "He's too drunk to steer a car. Knowing him, he probably misplaced the keys."

"Both of you are talking about me as though I'm not here." Francisco whipped off his aviators, exposing bloodshot eyes. He shrugged into his shirt, taking his time, fumbling with each button. "She's an expert and knows what she's doing." He swayed, and Krystal eyeballed the empty wine bottle. He'd consumed an epic amount of liquor.

All six feet two inches of Adolfo's wrath landed on Francisco. "Why did you risk Krystal's life by bringing her to Medão Beach?"

"Why are *you* seeing Isabel when you know how important she is to me?"

"This isn't about Isabel. It's about Krystal."

Francisco's expression radiated cockiness, although he stood six inches shorter than Adolfo. "Is it? Or is it about how you think you can get any woman you choose? When Isabel finds out I was at the beach with a world-famous surfer and your latest love interest, she'll come back to me."

Before Krystal had time to react to the news that Francisco had used her to provoke the woman he claimed to love, Francisco said, "By the way, you're fitting the role perfectly, Adolfo."

"What role?"

"The role of a tyrant like your father."

Adolfo's muscles bunched beneath his gray T-shirt. "What did you say?"

Francisco pointed a thick index finger straight toward Adolfo's face. Too close. Krystal knew Adolfo wouldn't like it, but Francisco's conception of personal space was conveniently nonexistent.

"You're marking a never-ending report card. No one can reach your lofty standards," Francisco said.

"Leave. Now." Right before Krystal's eyes, the soft-spoken Adolfo she'd known since that first day at the cottage had been replaced by a seething, furious Adolfo.

Neither man had ever acted like a raging bear before, compelling Krystal to either dash for cover or physically separate them. Fortified by her exasperation at the universe in general, she used her board as a barrier between them. "Stop. Stop. Both of you."

"Whatever you wish, *senhorita*." Francisco retreated quickly, stomping and stumbling, carting himself off as if he had something to prove.

Adolfo caught her by the shoulders. "Give up this absurd path you're bent on. Do it for me."

She dropped her surfboard into the sand. The ocean air she loved so much was fragmented by his statement.

*Adolfo, please understand. How can I choose? I love you and want to please you. I also need to prove to myself that I'm a winner. I've held onto this dream for so long.*

The briny depths of the ocean churned; seagulls skipped along the chaotic waves. The wind blew persistently, those fat gray clouds amassing into the beginnings of a thunderstorm.

"All I've ever known is surfing," she said quietly.

"I'm warning you for the last time. Do not surf. It's too dangerous."

She balked at his commanding tone. "Must you overthink every situation? Can't you be spontaneous like Francisco?"

"I swear, if you ever say his name again—"

"You'll what? Prevent me from becoming a winner? If so, let me congratulate you for accomplishing your goal so admirably."

He stared down at her. Nope, no warm chocolate-fudge gaze there, still a sizzling green. "Someone must protect you from yourself."

A couple smudges of dirt were on his cheeks, a dark stubble on his strong jaw. He was the man who worked the land.

She almost reached out to stroke the dirt from his cheeks, to calm the worry in his gaze, but she didn't deserve to touch him, to comfort him, anymore. She'd betrayed his belief in her that she'd be sensible and do the right thing. Had she ever been worthy of a man like him?

"You're successful," she said. "Let me be successful like you." Her voice cracked.

"I'm a far cry from success."

"Your father may have led you to believe otherwise, but you are brilliant and will succeed." She blew out an frustrated breath. "He must have praised you once in a while."

Judging from Adolfo's impassive expression, that had never happened.

He planted his feet wide. "This is the end of any conversation about my father."

"Can't you deal with the world when it doesn't spin your way?" She whipped her towel up from the sand. "My American driver's license is valid in Portugal and I'll drive Francisco's car back to the cottage."

"Your decision to leave without talking this out is unwise, Krystal. I suggest you reconsider very carefully."

"Is this your idea of asking me to stay? I'm sorry you don't like my observations regarding your father."

His shrug proclaimed aloofness. "What about you, fussing over *your* father like he's a child?"

"He's always been there for me and I'm going to be there for him. One of the nurses from rehab said he's becoming forgetful. He can't live alone any longer."

"He won't be alone at the senior facility. He'll be surrounded by friends. And he's happy."

*He's happy. Present tense.*

She moved backward. Tiny grains of sand blew around her face, and her skin prickled. "How do you know he's happy?"

"Julio and your father rang me this morning."

"Rang *you?* Why didn't they call me?"

"They wanted to speak to me and Veronica gave them my number."

Her cheeks warmed to crimson. "How dare you go behind my back?"

"I didn't. Your father moved into the senior facility last week. They were concerned you'd be disappointed and wanted my input."

"You withheld this information from me? While I begged to surf again and again?"

"I found out this morning. Now you won't need the money from any winnings."

"Suppose I want to surf because I want to show *myself* that I can win?"

"You're here. I'm here. Your father is happy. That's all that matters."

"That's not all that matters to *me*." She removed her wetsuit and dragged on her jersey and sweatpants. "I'm surfing in the finals on Friday."

"I won't support you. Meet me on my terms."

"Or what?"

He shrugged.

Roughly, she seized her surf bag and zipped it closed. "So now our relationship is conditional? I either abide by your wishes, or else?"

Veronica appeared over the dunes, shouting and waving. She raced to Krystal, a polka-dotted kerchief tied askew around her hair, her tiered, ruffled skirt reaching her ankles. Her cheeks were smeared with off-kilter red blush. "Thank goodness you're all right. Adolfo finished early in Évora and stopped by my house on his way to your cottage. He flew out so fast after I told him Francisco had called, I jumped into my car to follow him and left the boys with Clemente." She glanced briefly at Adolfo, then at the surfboard and bag Krystal had picked up. "Are you leaving?"

"Yes, with Francisco. I expect he's sleeping off the liquor in his car." Although Krystal was furious with Francisco, he was her ride back to the cottage.

"If you came with him in that flashy red convertible, he isn't there. He probably wandered to one of the local pubs, so I'll bring you to the cottage. Settled?"

Forced into agreement, Krystal said yes. "Although on Friday, I'm competing," she added. "I'm a wildcard, and this chance to surf in the finals comes once in a lifetime."

Veronica reared back. "Is a serious brain injury worth a few thousand dollars?"

Purposely slow, Krystal hoisted her surf gear. "It's no longer about the money."

"It's about a free-for-all nonsense sport that might get you killed." Adolfo's quelling frown seemed to silenced the air. Barely a leaf stirred, the wind buttoned up. "This is my last word of warning. No surfing. Call it a recommendation, if you will."

Recommendation? His voice brooked no argument.

Krystal pushed back her shoulders. "I never excelled at obeying a dictator's orders."

"Forget surfing. Leave it in your past where it belongs."

Her throat constricted and she forced back tears. There was only one thing she was going to forget. Him. Because after Friday, she was saying goodbye to Portugal and Adolfo forever.

For a split second, she thought he might pull her back as she shoved by, imagined his plea. *Don't leave, Krystal. Carry on. I'm here for you, in sickness and in health ...*

He didn't say a word. Not one word. Nothing.

And neither did she, for anything she said would be wrong.

She wanted to tell him that her whole being lightened whenever he gazed at her. She wanted to tell him that her heart was finally, irrevocably broken with the choice he'd forced her to make.

She thought of Rhode Island and her typical snowy Christmases.

She thought of lush, steamy Portugal, and the delights of a holiday in a country still unknown to her.

*It's too much. Don't look back, don't come apart in front of him. You've lost everything important in your life. Winning is all that's left.*

# CHAPTER 18

"*Y*ou weren't talkative during the drive," Veronica said when they arrived at Krystal's cottage. Veronica shut off the car's ignition, although she made no move to get out.

Krystal shrugged. "There's nothing to say."

Daylight waned through the canopy of olive trees. Silvery-green leaves turned in the balmy breeze, and there was no sign of the earlier impending storm.

"Hmm. I think you have a lot to say." Veronica tapped her pink manicured fingers on the steering wheel. "Although I'll admit Adolfo has a bit of temper when his buttons are pushed."

"You mean when things don't go his way."

"He's worried about you, and understandably so."

"His concerns aren't necessary. I don't need him to take care of me." *My self-image has suffered enough.*

"Forgive my prying, but what is your relationship with him?"

Krystal hesitated and pulled her terry cloth jacket tighter

around her. "Our relationship is developing. *Was* developing."

"He cares a great deal about you, more than he cares to admit, even to himself."

"Wrong topic, Veronica." Determined to remain aloof, Krystal let her gaze wander aimlessly, taking in the faded orange bougainvillea dripping over the front porch trellis. "As long as I obey his wishes, he'll continue to see me. Meanwhile, he met another woman for lunch today, the famed 'Miss Portugal.'"

"I don't believe it. And if he did, it's because her parents own a winery near Lisbon. Adolfo mentioned he might purchase supplies from them, which is why he's met with her before. So there, you're wrong. Besides, I see the way he looks at you."

Krystal glanced at her cell phone, which had pinged repeatedly during the drive. Adolfo's number blinked on the screen.

She shoved her phone in her purse and covered her face with her hands. She refused to listen to his messages, wouldn't read his texts. Because if she did, she'd cry. And if she cried, she wouldn't be able to stop.

Veronica squeezed her shoulder. "Are you okay?"

Krystal shook off Veronica's hand and managed a half-hearted smile. "Please don't. I know you mean well."

Veronica blew the air out of her cheeks. "Well, anyway, I wanted to tell you before now … But, you had a lot to process between hearing about your father's move to the senior facility and your argument with Adolfo."

"Tell me what?" In the stingy light of dusk, Krystal corralled her gear and exited the car as Veronica started for the cottage. A television set hummed from inside.

Krystal blinked. She hadn't left the television on. In fact, she hadn't watched any TV since arriving in Portugal.

An elegantly coiffed woman wearing fuchsia-colored lipstick opened the door. Her shiny black hair was shot with gray tips. Her dimples winked with her welcoming smile. She came to the porch's steps and extended her hand. "I'm Edite Silva. You must be Krystal. I've heard so much about you."

"As I was about to say," Veronica filled in rapidly, with a glance in Krystal's direction. "Aunt Edite stays at the cottage in December and runs the cash register in our family store during the Christmas season. She's the talented artist I told you about, remember?"

Krystal set down her gear and shook the older woman's hand. "Oh, it's a pleasure to meet you, Ms. ....?"

"Silva. I never married. My brother, who recently passed, was Clemente and Adolfo's father."

Aunt Edite smelled of paints and canvas, her manner saturating the air with color and kindness.

"I'm sorry for your loss." Krystal glanced at Veronica. "For both your losses."

"My brother and I weren't close," Aunt Edite said, "although I always spent Christmas with him and his family. This holiday will be our first without him. We'll set an extra plate at the table for *alminhas a penar*." At Krystal's inquiring glance, she clarified, "'The souls of the dead.' We offer a food gift to ensure they will do well in the future." She linked arms with Krystal and guided her inside the cottage. "In any event, the loss of a loved one is difficult, especially during the holidays. Men don't show their emotions the way women do, although I'm certain both Clemente and Adolfo are struggling with their grief."

Veronica picked up Krystal's surfing gear and deposited it inside the cottage. "Clemente has immersed himself in his office work since his father's death. I've hardly seen him."

"Typical male response," Aunt Edite said with a heart-

117

ening smile. "Continue to be there for your husband. Everyone mourns in their own way."

Krystal took a silent, pained breath. Besides his endless work demands, Adolfo was swamped with sorrow. This was a difficult season in his life, and she'd made their relationship all about her and her selfish demands.

"We'll be roommates, and I moved my luggage into the upstairs loft," Aunt Edite was saying.

"Please, I don't want to put you to any trouble," Krystal said.

"Aside from the fact that I'm forty years older than you, I'm still spry." Aunt Edite's dark-lashed almond-shaped eyes scrutinized Krystal. "I can see why you're a surfer. You're so tall and thin."

"What I meant is, I won't be in Portugal after Friday. I'm booking my airline ticket back to Rhode Island."

"Well, that's my cue to leave." Veronica rubbed her palms over her skirt and then glanced at her wristwatch. "I have to check on the twins to be sure my house is still intact, so I'll leave you two to get acquainted and ring you tomorrow."

Aunt Edite nodded. "I stopped at the market in Évora on my way here. *Caldo verde*, kale soup, is simmering on the stove. Krystal and I are two capable women and are all set for the night."

"No surprise there. You always have everything under control." Veronica waved a cheerful good-bye followed by a hasty exit.

Aunt Edite nabbed Krystal's elbow and led her to the kitchen. "Let's be blessed with a delicious dinner and have a heart-to-heart talk."

Krystal glanced downward. "I may not be up to a heart-to-heart anything."

"Then I'll talk. It's my favorite pastime. By the way,

cooked rice and a pudding recipe were left on the kitchen countertop."

"Right. I intended to—"

"From what I understand, you were preoccupied today at the beach. No worries. I prepared the pudding."

Krystal sniffed the mouth-watering scent of smoked sausage and kale. Normally, she didn't eat kale, preferring a thick hamburger and French fries. Today, she found the strong cabbage aroma comforting.

While Krystal set the table, Aunt Edite slid onto a stool and snapped up a pencil and paper napkin.

Noting the quick strokes, Krystal peered over Aunt Edite's shoulder. "May I ask what you're drawing?"

"I'm drawing you. If I added color, your eyes would be a flash of blue. And your hair is magnificent. You must have a mile of it."

"No one's ever drawn me before. I'm sketching, or rather, trying to sketch, swim designs for my yet-to-be-named swimsuit company."

Aunt Edite focused on Krystal's face, then went back to her pencil and napkin. "May I see your sketches sometime? I'll offer a helping hand, if you'd like."

"Certainly. Yes, thank you, and I'd be eternally grateful. I'll show you the sketches tomorrow."

With a nod, Aunt Edite pushed back her stool. Taking the thick creamy soup off the heat, she ladled potatoes, sausage, and kale into speckled-blue pottery bowls and placed a basket of crusty bread on the kitchen table. She settled into the seat across from Krystal and prayed a simple grace.

Lively conversation accompanied their meal, and Krystal scarcely believed an hour had passed by the time she'd cleared the soup bowls and brewed a pot of herbal tea.

Aunt Edite set the rice pudding on the table, then sat and

perched her chin on her slim folded hands. "So, you won't be joining us for Christmas?"

Krystal sank into the white-tiled chair across from Aunt Edite. "No."

"What a shame. I could use help in the retail store, and Christmas Day is such fun with Bento and Bernardo. Portuguese tradition accords that the Three Wise Men, not Santa Claus, bring the gifts on Christmas Eve."

Unable to get comfortable, Krystal crossed and uncrossed her legs. "All your holiday traditions are fascinating."

"Indeed. And Christmas is one of the most magical. I've celebrated Christmas with the Silva family since Clemente and Adolfo were boys."

"What was Adolfo like when he was a boy?"

Aunt Edite smiled. "One Christmas in particular is fixed in my mind, when Adolfo was a toddler. He played for hours with a toy train set, designing and redesigning the tracks round and round the Christmas tree. He was very creative, and solved the smallest of problems in unique ways. He wanted to be an architect."

Krystal nodded, imagining a dark-haired boy, his nose a tad crooked, most likely tall for his age, his wide hazel eyes brimming with complexity beyond his years.

She dragged herself from her musings. "Any boyhood transgressions?"

Aunt Edite sipped her tea. "There was the time when he was ten years old and didn't come home for Christmas lunch. I still remember whiffs of the stuffed turkey baking in the oven before the family realized he'd been gone too long. We all went outside and combed the farm looking for him."

"Where was he?"

"Much to his parents' dismay, he'd snuck out early in the morning to design and build an elaborate fort. He was posi-tively covered in dirt by the time we all came running up.

With a pile of twigs in one hand and plans for the fort he'd drawn up in the other, he gaped at us, probably wondering what all the fuss was about."

"Should I laugh or cry?"

"His mother wept with relief at finding him. His father, however, delivered a deafening rant regarding Adolfo's rash and reckless behavior. Even though it was Christmas, Adolfo was sent to his room."

Krystal plucked up a napkin and dabbed at her eyes. The thought of Adolfo as an exuberant child with high expectations, and then the hard-working man he'd become, the man who'd shouldered his duties without hesitation, brought a dull throb to her chest.

Aunt Edite reached out and touched her hand. "Christmas carolers came to the door later that evening, and Adolfo was allowed out of his room. He immediately went to his father and hugged him. That boy always had a heart of compassion."

"He cares for everyone around him."

Astuteness shone from the elderly woman's eyes. "And he's smitten with you."

"You couldn't be more wrong."

"I'm never mistaken about my nephew. He and I lunched in Évora today. He laughed out loud and seemed content and happy for the first time in a long while. I'd feared he'd never come to grips with his father's death. His father was so tough on him, and, as Adolfo matured, he began to argue back, and rightfully so."

Krystal's napkin dropped to the floor. "*You* were his luncheon date?"

"Didn't he tell you?" Aunt Edite helped herself to a heaping tablespoon of rice pudding directly from the pot and grimaced.

"No, he didn't." Krystal twisted her wristwatch. "We had a

terrible row at the beach and I split." She'd left first, before he had the opportunity to leave her.

"In Évora, I helped him purchase a Christmas gift for you, and an ornament for the top of your Christmas tree."

Vigorously, Krystal shook her head. "It's not my tree, Ms. Silva."

"Please, call me Aunt Edite. From what I gathered, you'll soon be part of the family."

Krystal studied her cup of tepid chamomile tea. "He can't seem to understand my need to prove myself."

"One of my favorite pastors once said, 'The most important story is the one you tell yourself.'"

Krystal linked her fingers together. "Do you want to hear my story? I'm a champion surfer."

Aunt Edite wagged her spoon. "There's more to life than that."

"My father is waiting for me in Rhode Island."

Setting down her spoon, Aunt Edite place her hand over Krystal's linked fingers. "Adolfo mentioned your devotion to your father. Although admirable, perhaps you've limited yourself. There is a man here in Portugal who needs you. Don't exclude him from your life."

In her bedroom later that evening, Krystal set her surfing gear by her nightstand, and smoothed her fingers over her surfboard. She loved the smells of the ocean, the wet wood and salty fish, the sense that the world was just waiting for her to achieve her goals.

"Angel, I must surf in the finals. You're the only one that understands how far we've come to reach this goal."

The scent of the ever-burning oak log, blending with

fragrances of pine, seeped through her closed bedroom door. The scents of Christmas in Portugal.

Setting Angel aside, she padded to the window, opened it, and rested her hip on the sill. Fresh, cool breezes flooded the room, entering her as the inspiration for a new life. For a moment, she closed her eyes and absorbed the night sounds of Portugal—the peal of church bells, the chirping of noisy crickets, a dog barking somewhere in the distance.

She glanced at the woven wool rug covering her bedroom floor. Her first night at the cottage, she'd hunched over that rug with the lights off and suffered the worst headache of her life.

She retraced her first days in Portugal—her wipeout and resultant concussion, Adolfo's reassuring, subdued voice while he spoke to her in Portuguese. Always, her thoughts veered to him, his sizzling hazel gaze when he kissed her, the scruff of his dark beard against her cheek, his thick black hair, casual and careless after a day's work.

Despite her craving for all things Adolfo, why would she change her goals, her lifestyle, to suit him? All those years perfecting her techniques. All those sacrifices.

If she participated in the finals, he'd made it clear he wouldn't want to see her again. Her ambitions meant little to him. And if she didn't participate? Well, then, inch by inch, she'd lose her foothold on everything she'd once deemed important.

Her heart thudded hard in her chest. Her conflicting thoughts threatened to break the dam holding back her tears.

She crossed to her nightstand, retrieved her cell phone, and pressed *play* to hear Adolfo's voicemail messages.

His baritone voice resonated into the silence.

*Krystal, please answer the phone.*

*Krystal, answer the phone.*

And she read and reread his text messages:

*Next time I call, pick up your worthless cell phone.*

Followed by: *I'll text you tomorrow. Please, we need to talk.*

"I make my own path and live by it," she whispered. Yet, her loneliness was bottomless without him.

She stared at the phone. She wanted to call him. Of course, she didn't. Instead, she set the phone on her nightstand and ran her fingers along her leather-embossed sketch pad.

Aunt Edite was a talented artist and successful entrepreneur. Could she bring Krystal's visions, her swimsuit designs, to reality? Could Krystal leave her dusty story behind and find a new life, a happier Christmas, in Portugal? Could the despair from her repeated abandonments be assuaged by Adolfo's love?

She shook off the inertia accompanying her conflicting emotions. The soft woolen blanket on her bed had been turned down, probably by the thoughtful Aunt Edite. With a weighty sigh, Krystal slid beneath the blanket and shut her eyes. Sleep would enable her to consider her future in a clearer light.

Daylight wasn't near when she woke. A full winter moon rode high in a charcoal sky smeared with gray. She rolled onto her stomach, chasing the truce of slumber before she lost it to an endless night of tossing and turning, and the anguishing dilemmas plaguing her.

# CHAPTER 19

*A*t precisely eleven o'clock in the morning on Friday, December nineteenth, Krystal let her gaze roam over Medão Beach. The Atlantic Ocean sparkled, crashing against the shore. Beachgoers in bathing suits sat cross-legged on the blistering sand. A mild sea breeze carrying scents of coconut suntan lotion and salt water brushed through her hair.

She lifted her face to the comforting warmth of the sun. People called Portugal the edge of Europe. To her, this incomparable country was the center of her heart.

Spectators, each rooting for their favorite contestants, mingled along the sloping rise. This modest fishing town was splendid, resembling a picture book of laughter and sunbeams.

And she felt so alone. The special event held no sign of a tall, ruggedly handsome man with compassionate hazel eyes.

Surely Veronica had told Adolfo of Krystal's decision.

And Krystal had hoped, a small, quiet hope, that he would show up to support her. But he hadn't. He hadn't bothered to call nor text.

It took every bit of her self-control to turn away from the spectators, to rest her hands silently on her surfboard.

As she waited for her heat to be called, Sam Larson came to stand beside her.

"Thanks again for bringing me to the surfing finals," she said. "I'm sorry for phoning you last minute. I was undecided about today."

Below bleached-blond brows, Sam's green-eyed gaze zeroed in on her. "More than glad to help out a champ. We were all wondering where you disappeared to, and then I find you've been staying on an olive farm of all places. Are you ready to win this heat by a landslide?"

She glanced at the ocean, and her mouth went dry. If only time would speed up and the heat was over.

"I managed to surf once since my concussion, and it didn't go well," she said.

He crossed his arms. "Then should you surf today? Concussions and surfing don't mix."

"The World Surf League deemed me worthy enough to be granted another opportunity. Otherwise, I didn't qualify." Krystal gestured to the curvaceous Wilhelmina, who'd already completed a successful surf. "She's in the lead for the women's events."

Sam whistled through his teeth. "Yes she is."

"And you're in the lead for the men."

"A double hurrah for me."

"Double?"

A dazzling white smile wreathed his face. "Wilhelmina and I are together."

"As in dating?'

With a decisive clunk, Sam planted the nose of his surfboard into the sand, and then leaned against it. "Ever since I congratulated her on her win at the Peniche preliminaries, we've dated. We're flying back to the States on Sunday."

She grinned. "The media will love a jaw-dropping, glamorous surfing couple. You'll get plenty of sponsorships."

"We're counting on it. When are you traveling back to Rhode Island?"

Krystal's assigned heat blasted through the announcer's bullhorn and she didn't have time to answer Sam. Wearing a pasted-on smile, she attached her surf leash, swept up her surfboard and sprinted to the ocean's edge.

Surfers emerging from the water warned of a rip current, and how even the strongest swimmer could be swept out to sea.

She paused in midstep.

*Rip currents are drowning machines.*

Please, please, anything but that. She'd warned Ernie not to surf that fateful day, pleaded with him. Intent on pursuing his own interests and disregarding everyone else's opinion, including hers, he'd opted for his surfboard. Nevertheless, she should have insisted. Why hadn't she insisted?

Ignoring the phantom pain in her wrist, she flexed and unflexed her fingers. All of a sudden, conditions seemed windier, the sea churned rougher, the water murky and foamy.

Her heartbeat went erratic. Dizzy, she leaned over and put her head between her knees. Conceivably, the spectators would think she was limbering up. The blood raced to her head, emboldening her.

Lightly, she patted Angel. *Don't be scared. You need to see this through. If conditions were dangerous, the officials would have canceled the competition.*

She threw down an invisible gauntlet, determined to overcome her fears, ignoring the butterflies taking up permanent residence in her stomach. With a long-held breath, she mounted her surfboard and paddled into the icy waters of the Atlantic Ocean.

* * *

STEPS away from a rocky enclave at the far end of Medão Beach's shoreline, Adolfo stood stiffly with Veronica. Bento and Bernardo were sandwiched between them. Why he'd agreed to Veronica's suggestion that she follow him to the beach in her own car, her ever-talkative twins in tow, was beyond him.

"Krystal's an expert surfer." Veronica's smile came easy as she kissed one son's hair, then the other's. "She'll be so happy when she realizes you're here."

"I sincerely doubt it."

A gleam appeared in Veronica's eyes. "Believe me, Krystal will be delighted."

Krystal. The only woman he'd ever loved didn't love him. She had come to Portugal with a surfboard and rigid aspirations, and, less than a week ago, she had been softer, brighter, when he'd held her. He'd never anticipated finding a woman like her. She was brave, too brave for her own good, with bewitching blue eyes. A woman who loved chocolate, and Christmas, and believed in angels.

He watched as she stood near the shore, holding her surfboard. Firmly, he gripped the twins' shoulders as they giggled and wrapped their arms around Veronica's legs.

He rolled his shoulders in a vain attempt to shrug off his tension. "Nonetheless, I'm here to support Krystal, and to pull her out of the water if anything goes wrong."

Veronica pivoted as the boys ducked beneath Adolfo and streaked toward a nearby hot dog stand. "I brought some towels and a pail, and I'll settle the boys underneath a beach umbrella. Hot dogs will keep them occupied, at least for a while." She laughed affectionately at the twins, already halfway to the hot dog stand. "After Krystal's surf event, we'll leave. I assume you're sticking around?"

"*Sim.*" Adolfo eyed the rough Atlantic. Suppose Krystal floundered in that churning water? Suppose she went under, and the waves sucked up every bit of her precious oxygen? He rubbed a hand over his heart, his stance restless. "I can't watch. I'm not suited to standing idle."

"You can't pull her out of the water if you're not watching," Veronica called over her shoulder.

He snatched up the twins' pail. "Believe me, I'll be listening to the announcer's every word."

Farther down the beach, he filled the pail with water. Hauling the pail a few feet up the beach, he knelt, immersed his arms elbow-deep in sand, and started digging. He should build Krystal something impressive, something special and exquisite, while he waited for her.

Once, when he heard her name being called by the announcer, he viewed her. Only once. Although she effortlessly glided through the water on her surfboard, his breath hung in his throat.

He went back to the sand.

On this very same beach, he'd demanded that she choose between him and her sport. Barring the fact that he disagreed with her views on surfing, who was he to stop her? She was a widow and had fended for herself for several years. She'd lost her mother and had endured tremendous sadness at a young age.

What if he had told her that she could surf, but that he'd trusted she wouldn't because he was too afraid of the outcome—of losing her. Would she have responded to his relentless phone calls and texts then, before he'd decided to ease off and give her a couple days to think about their disagreement? What if he'd *asked* her to reconsider competing, instead of issuing an ultimatum?

All week, he hadn't been able to switch off the "what ifs," although he'd tried, burying himself in his farm work, seeking any distraction. His father's maxim had flown through his mind.

Work, work, work.

So Adolfo had pruned, and planted, all the while thinking exclusively of her.

That infernal bullhorn again, announcing the next heat. He peered up. He didn't know anything about surfing, although by the ebb and flow of the crowd and their reaction, she hadn't surfed well.

"Adolfo?"

His heart stopped beating at the sound of Krystal's voice. How many minutes had gone by? He lost the capacity to breathe as his gaze fixed on her.

"Adolfo, you came to the beach to watch me surf? Veronica was at the water's edge and just told me." Krystal's face was flushed, her eyes huge and blue.

"You sound like you can't catch your breath," he said.

"I've been running—trying to find you."

His gaze stayed on her, only on her. The sight of her, her striped towel thrown over her shoulder, still wearing her form-fitting wetsuit, jolted his insides with an electric current. Never had she looked so gorgeous, or so peaceful. She was a glimmer of sunshine moving toward him, glistening wet with droplets of ocean water streaming down her face.

He didn't stand.

Was she delighted to see him? Was she disappointed?

Keeping his fingers occupied, he continued sifting double handfuls of cool sand, applying a fair amount of water to help the sand stick together. Hadn't she said something about good quality sand containing no rocks? This sand was loaded with tiny pebbles.

She leaned her hands on her knees. "What are you building?"

He wanted her to grin, to see her infectious smile when he was finished. He wanted her to think of this moment, of him, always.

"It's a surprise." He wanted to say more. His words were enmeshed in the blue sky, in the relentless surf, in her nearness.

* * *

"SURPRISES SEEM TO BE YOUR SPECIALITY." Krystal knelt beside Adolfo and drizzled a small amount of water into the sand.

Adolfo drew a labored breath, gave a curt nod. All potent vitality and attractive masculinity.

At first, she'd wondered if he'd heard her when she approached, although he'd stared at her before turning back to his sand sculpture. When she'd finally found him on this far end of the beach, she'd felt a stab of desire so great that her knees had weakened. He was so grand, so impressive in his fitted gray T-shirt and jeans. If he'd only look at her again, tease her with a genial smile rather than being so absorbed, she'd wrap her arms around his hard, muscular shoulders and plead with him.

Plead with him for what exactly? Forgiveness? Understanding? Patience?

Sand spilled through her fingers. "You found some decent quality sand. It should be a little finer, though."

"All I could find."

He was certainly occupied with whatever he was making.

She added more water to pack the sand firmer. "You need to smooth out the edges of your sculpture once it gets higher. Where's the kitchen spatula?"

"Forgot it."

She snuck a peek at him. His dark stubble was thicker than usual. His gaze was lowered beneath his dark lashes.

The noonday sun emphasized his dark tan and the minute creases on his forehead and near his lips. Creases of hard work, of levity, of worry. His Mediterranean nature was innate—tempers deeply experienced and strongly contained.

She pulled in some air. "I didn't surf well. I lost the heat."

"I know." His hands stopped, then started again. "Despite your loss, I'm proud of all you've accomplished. You surfed extremely well."

"How do you know? You've been building castles in the sand."

He smiled, but not at her. His gaze remained fixed on his task. "It's not a castle."

"When I heard talk from the other surfers about rip currents, I—I was afraid." She flashed a peek at the ocean. "I faced my fears."

He looked up. His hazel gaze had changed from anguish-shadowed green to something richer. A deliciously warm hot fudge. "Since we've met, I've regarded you as the most courageous person I've ever known."

Blood hummed through her veins. He was finally acknowledging her, not seeming hundreds of miles away.

"And I learned something else—something important about myself this morning," she couldn't resist continuing. "The in-law apartment I wanted to build for my dad was more to assuage my guilt for not being there for him these past three years, rather than for him. I believed that I'd neglected him after Ernie's death to nurse my own wounds. And I did. Dad and I spoke on the phone last evening and he's forgiven me—although he assured me there was nothing to forgive. So, I confronted my faults and failures, and I forgave myself. Nobody's perfect."

"*You* are."

She shook her head. "I'm far from perfect."

"When will you be traveling back to America?"

"I'm not. My dad is the happiest he's been in a long time, and the Senior Lifestyle Facility is planning a big Christmas celebration. He's on the decorating committee, and has made lots of new friends."

Adolfo's hands paused in the sand as he looked up, his expression stunned. "You're spending Christmas in Portugal?"

"Aunt Edite asked me to help her in the Silva family store. In turn, she's sketching my swimsuit designs. The woman is a gifted artist. We're roommates."

"Not for long." Their gazes came together, hers and Adolfo's, private and swift. Her pulse flittered. He was so close, the scent of soil and earth clinging to his clothes, even here at the beach.

"What do you mean?" she asked, daring him to continue.

He brushed the sand off his hands and cupped her face, his breath whispering against her temple. "You're coming home with me."

"I don't understand."

"Try this." He embraced her, his arms warm and strong through her wetsuit. "Krystal Walters, will you marry me?"

"You mean right here in the middle of the beach?"

"I'll give you a couple of weeks to plan the wedding. Do you want me to ask you to marry me on my knees?"

"You already are." She grinned. She'd missed him so much, the feel of his calloused hands, his breathtaking smile.

"Well?"

She snuggled nearer, her arms winding around his shoulders. She wanted everything about him. "Adolfo Silva, the answer is *sim*, I will marry you. *Sim, sim, sim.*"

Aunt Edite was right. There was more to life than surfing, and that included Adolfo.

He brushed his lips over her hair. She tilted her head to

gaze at him and her heart kicked. Oh, how she loved this powerful, charismatic man.

He crushed her against his chest. His lips on hers were moist and earnest. When he finally tore his mouth away, he settled his forehead against hers. The moisture from his sweat melded with the dampness of her wet hair.

"That's settled then." He stood and assisted her to her feet, brushed the sand from her wetsuit. His fingers lingered on her hands. "Krystal?"

She faced him, cautious of his reproach because she'd ignored the doctor's advice and had surfed. Adolfo hadn't mentioned it. Surely, he would. The subject needed to be broached.

"I won't prevent you from surfing again, if that's what you want to do." His voice was quiet, his eyes downcast. "Is that what you want?"

She turned and gazed at the ocean. One last look. Scores of seabirds squawked and swooped through the heavens before plunging into the water for fish. Clouds covered the normally blue sky. The beach breeze had turned chilly on her skin. A light, foamy mist sprayed her face, a gentle farewell.

"Not all dreams are meant for a lifetime," she said. "New dreams take their place. Better dreams."

"Either way, I will support whatever you choose."

Arching a brow, she grinned. "Really?"

"As long as I don't have to watch." His solid arms closed around her. "Krystal Walters, I love you so much."

She attempted to repay his smile with one of her own. Instead, she blinked back tears. "I love you, too."

He cradled her face, stroked the tears from her cheeks. "Then why are you crying?"

"Because when I decided to surf in the finals, I assumed I'd never hear you say those words."

He hugged her. "I loved you this morning, last night, last week. And I love you now more than ever."

Everyone deserved a second chance at love, especially at Christmas.

She grasped her striped towel. "I'm officially retiring my lucky towel, although it wasn't so lucky after all."

"I disagree. That towel made me the luckiest man in the world, because it brought you to Portugal."

She smiled and straightened her shoulders. She could still smell the salt from the ocean as he guided her away from the beach. The spectators had disbanded. The finals had ended. The shore had emptied.

"Let's get your surfing gear and go back to the olive farm."

She paused and swung around. "You never told me about your sand sculpture. What were you building?"

And then she understood. She could see the heart-shaped face, the doe-like eyes, the wings.

An angel.

# CHAPTER 20

Krystal layered boiled, sliced potatoes onto the boiled and shredded salted cod. In another baking dish, she added sautéed onions, black olives and hard-boiled eggs. "My first Christmas Eve supper in Portugal," she declared.

Veronica smiled. "Your first of many *Consoadas*." She wiped her hands on her frilly green apron adorned with mistletoe and then tended to flash-boiling an array of shellfish, including crab, clams, and pink shrimp. She arranged the seafood on a white ceramic platter to serve warm in their shells. "How's this?"

"Looks delicious," Krystal said. "Truly, I've never seen so much food."

The women paraded into Veronica's expansive dining room. The shiny mahogany table fairly groaned beneath an assortment of hazelnuts, olives and garden-fresh collard greens drizzled in olive oil.

Krystal peeked at her reflection in the hallway mirror as she passed. She'd fussed with her appearance, wearing her hair in a side-swept chignon and donning a candy-apple-red crepe shift she'd purchased in Peniche, along with black kitten heels.

Aunt Edite placed a silver candelabrum, lit with a half dozen red and green candles, in the center of the table. "*Consoada* literally translated means 'to comfort.' Traditionally, we abstain from meat dishes on Christmas Eve because Advent is our 'little lent' and we fast and repent the days before Christmas."

"Until Christmas Day," Adolfo added, "when pork and roasted lamb are served."

He had stood as the women marched into the room. He was so strikingly handsome, Krystal thought, so unbearably splendid, wearing a linen shirt and gray dress pants. His thick, wavy black hair framed his face.

He strode to her and claimed her with a kiss. "*Boas Festas,* beautiful." Arm in arm, he led her to her place at the table. As he seated her, he whispered in her ear. "After we attend Midnight Mass, *Missa do Galo,* I have a surprise for you."

"Surprises are your speciality."

"*Sim.*" He grinned sheepishly. "Gift giving is an important part of a Portuguese Christmas."

"I don't have a gift for you, Adolfo. I'm sorry. I'll buy you something when we fly to America to see my family."

"You're here in Portugal. That is my gift."

His oddly rough voice gave Krystal pause. The clean-air scent of him fused with the aromas of olive oil and pine trees and olives. Her spirits flooded with happiness, marveling at the sincere goodwill reflected on the faces of the Portuguese family she loved. *Her* family.

And her family in America who were also experiencing a wonderful holiday. She'd spoken to her brother and father earlier that evening. Her father was spending Christmas Eve with Julio's family, and Christmas Day would be enjoyed at the senior facility, where he'd perform in a Christmas carol concert, along with other residents. He'd discovered a love for singing.

She scanned the Silva family table, savoring the scene, tucking it away to reflect on for years to come. Clemente was seated at the head, Aunt Edite on his right and Veronica on his left. Krystal was next to Aunt Edite, and Adolfo took a seat across from Krystal. Bento and Bernardo sat on either side of Adolfo. At the other end of the table was an empty place set for Adolfo and Clemente's father, *alminhas a penar.*

After they bowed their heads and said grace, Clemente poured red wine into the adults' glasses and sparkling water for the children.

"Uncle Adolfo said that Bento and I should behave and be extra good tonight," Bernardo said, "so that Father Christmas will put presents in our *sapatinhos.* Those are shoes," he translated for Krystal. Despite Veronica's obvious attempts to slick down his wavy brown hair, it whirled upward in undisciplined wisps at the crown. "Is he right, Krystal ... I mean, Aunt Krystal? Uncle Adolfo said we should start calling you that."

She laughed. "Absolutely."

"Aunt Krystal, do you know that Christmas Eve is my favorite night of the year?" Bento asked. He reached for his water glass and knocked it over, spilling water onto the floor and Adolfo's shoes. He glanced up at Adolfo. "Sorry, Uncle Adolfo."

Adolfo ran his fingers through his hair, then set the glass upright. "No worries. I'll wear my work boots to church tonight. I always keep a spare here. You're a good boy and all is forgiven." He patted Bento's unruly brown hair, which grew in short spikes around his face.

Bento glanced at Veronica. "Sorry, Mom."

Clemente grimaced and Veronica smiled as she grabbed some napkins to wipe up the mess. "It's only water, dear."

Krystal gazed across the table at Adolfo. "Christmas Eve is my favorite too."

"And mine. And the Portuguese make Christmas Eve the longest night of the year."

Veronica dashed salt and a pinch of black pepper on the vegetables. "I never tell the boys when to go to bed on Christmas Eve."

"They play until they drop." Adolfo leaned back in his chair and regarded both boys. "Thus, the longest night of the year."

Along with a crack of laughter, Aunt Edite raised her glass of port. "*Bom apetite e Feliz Natal.* Good appetite and Merry Christmas!"

Conversation crisscrossed the table, along with the clinks of silverware and the clanks of chili-red glazed dinnerware. By the end of the meal, Adolfo had the boys giggling as he pretended to pull pennies out of their ears.

After they were finished, Clemente put down his fork and knife and addressed the table at large. "We'll leave for Midnight Mass within the hour."

After a last sip of coffee, Krystal assisted the family in clearing the dishes and setting the table for dessert. Veronica waltzed into the kitchen with her arms around the loves of her life—Clemente, Bento and Bernardo.

* * *

AFTER MIDNIGHT MASS, the family returned to Veronica and Clemente's home. In the formal living room, Clemente switched on the television set for a singalong with the *Coro de Santo,* the holy choir.

Bento and Bernardo hastened to their *sapatinhos* by the

fireplace, squealing with excitement as they opened their gifts.

Krystal abandoned her heels, hung her light cotton jacket in the foyer closet, and stifled a yawn with her hand.

"Tired?" Adolfo asked in a laughter-tinged voice. His gaze shifted to the wall-mounted clock chiming one a.m. "The night is young." He took her hand and led her to Clemente's study down the hall. Beside a bow window stood a miniature Christmas tree wrapped in twinkling white lights. An elaborate crèche displaying the three main figures of the nativity, Infant Jesus, Mary, and Joseph, sat beneath the tree.

"As you can see, we celebrate Christmas everywhere." Adolfo closed the door behind them. "Clemente, Veronica, and Aunt Edite will be awake for hours, unwrapping and setting up all the toys the twins received."

"Don't you want to join in the festivities?"

He grinned. "Later."

He sat beside her on a leather loveseat tucked into one corner of the wood-paneled room. A wool rug stretched across the tiled floor. He stared at Krystal, still scarcely believing that she was in Portugal.

She was here, after her courageous surf, when she'd been determined to win a contest she hadn't won. She was here, after fighting with him so fiercely.

How close he'd come to losing her because of his stubbornness, his inability to listen to anyone's side other than his own.

She had run through the crowd on Medão Grande Beach, intent on finding him after the surfing finals. And then she had stared at the ocean after he'd told her that he wouldn't stop her from surfing if that's what she wanted to do. After a long minute, she'd turned away from the sea, her chin lifted high. Then she'd taken his hand, apparently comfortable in the decision to leave her surfing life behind. Her huge blue eyes had shimmered with love and resolution.

Now she sat quietly, staring at the tree. The soft wash of Christmas lights illuminated her beautiful face.

He hooked an arm around her shoulders. "What are you thinking about?"

"You." She brushed back a wavy blonde strand of hair from her cheek.

He regarded the warmth in her gaze and grinned, both touched and pleased. A wave of tenderness for her gladdened him to the core. He'd come to her with a full heart and total commitment. He wanted to be sure she felt the same.

"Care to elaborate?" he asked.

A flicker of a smile touched her lips. "You know what impressed me most about you?"

"My work ethic?"

"Your crooked nose."

He laughed out loud. He couldn't help his reaction. He captured her in his arms, burying his face in the gardenia and vanilla scent of her hair.

She snuggled closer to his chest. "And I have a confession."

"This better be good. We just attended *Missa do Galo.*"

"And everything about the Mass was beautiful—the crib, walking up to the altar to kiss Baby Jesus, and the hymns we sang. The Portuguese appreciate the true meaning of Christmas."

"The season is meant to bring joy, and having you here to share it with me …" His mouth descended on hers.

"Adolfo—"

"I love when you say my name," he murmured, his lips still on hers.

"Remember my confession?"

Reluctantly, he lifted his head. "Of course. Please continue."

She drew an unsteady breath. A reddish tint, the color of a poinsettia, crept up her cheeks. "From the first day I saw you, I kept thinking, this is my love, my husband-to-be. He's here in Portugal. And then I'd think, no, that's impossible. He's high-handed and arrogant."

He chuckled. "Maybe sometimes."

"Many of the times I was railing at you because of your demands, I was distracted because I was thinking about you … kissing me."

"You mean like this?" He drew her nearer, his mouth moving with intensity over hers. It took all his effort to break the kiss, to compel his hands to stop caressing her exquisite figure. He shifted and rested his chin on her head. "Always, you were on my mind. And I have a confession, also."

She tipped up her chin. "I'm almost afraid to ask."

"The day I took you to the beach with the twins, you were dressed in a bikini with that black cover-up."

"I recall every detail of that day."

His lips traveled down her temples, lingering near her ears. "I kept hoping for a strong wind so I could catch more than a glimpse of your shapely legs beneath that cover-up. The weather didn't cooperate. If you remember, it was a clear, sunny day."

She grinned. "As usual."

He nuzzled her neck, muffling a laugh. "May I remind you that I have a gift for you."

"A chocolate bell to share?"

"Better." He reached into his shirt pocket and produced a small black velvet box. "I've carried this around with me since Aunt Edite and I shopped in Évora. Look inside."

Carefully, she opened the box. An exquisite diamond ring flashed, caught by the radiant lights of the Christmas tree.

"Adolfo." Her eyes welled with tears. "I've never seen a ring so beautiful. How?" She swallowed. "I remember Aunt Edite had mentioned you went shopping together."

Taking her left hand, he slid the ring onto her finger. "You and I will be married on January sixth."

"Less than two weeks from now?" She shook her head. "Impossible."

"It's perfect. Epiphany Eve is January fifth, so we'll marry the day after. We can get married at the beach you like—the one we took the twins to. I've already invited your family to the wedding and Veronica is arranging the flights. They arrive January first. After the wedding, we'll all fly to America so you can collect your belongings and return to Portugal to live in my home."

"They never said a word to me."

He smiled. "Surprise."

"I love being here in Portugal, although I'm sorry I wasn't able to spend Christmas with my father."

"In a way, you will." Adolfo threaded his fingers through the soft curls that had slipped from her upswept hair. "Epiphany Eve is another Christmas tradition. Bento and Bernardo will fill their shoes with carrots and straw and place them on the windowsill, because this will lure the Three Wise Men, who leave candied fruit and sweet bread. So your family can continue to celebrate the holiday along with us."

"Thank you for including my father in all your plans."

"I know how much he means to you."

"And I know how much your father meant to you," she said quietly.

"He carried an aura of control about him. Despite being feared for being such a hard taskmaster, he was respected."

JOSIE RIVIERA

"And you were the most considerate son a father could want. Despite disagreeing, you abided by your father's wishes. You're a hero because you always do the right thing."

"Please don't call me that. I'm just an overburdened man with a father who needed him." His denial had come out sharper than he'd intended. He softened his tone. "In hindsight, my father knew more about olive farming than I ever gave him credit for. Although …" His voice trailed off.

"Go on." Her blue eyes were compassionate. She was too attuned to his emotions.

He sighed. "Despite the work, I learned that life doesn't need to be so serious. I've put down my olive rake in order to truly enjoy Christmas and to love life again. You taught me about communication, about forgiveness. My shame I carried, arguing with my father before he died, couldn't find healing in an olive grove, nor in grape vines, nor in my attempts to close off the world and live alone. In the end, I couldn't succeed. Not without you." He covered her lips in an undemanding kiss.

"I'll help you establish your winery. That is, once I get my swimsuit company up and running."

"Aunt Edite is sketching your ideas?"

A faint crimson flush crept up her high cheekbones, the flush he loved, one of excitement and enthusiasm. "Yes. And I've finally decided on the perfect name."

He gazed down into her impossibly gorgeous face. Truly, this was a most perfect Christmas. "What is it?"

"When I realized how much I would miss you if I ever left Portugal, I decided on my company name. Aunt Edite agreed. So, you want to hear what it is?"

"*Sim.*" He closed his eyes, but he already knew.

"*Saudade,* because I love you so much."

It was a noun, not a verb, and unique to Portugal. A longing for, a yearning.

In aching tenderness, he snuggled her closer. "And I love you."

And he added another word connected to *saudade*. She didn't know the word yet, but he did.

*Fado.* Their destiny. It was simply the way it was.

**THE END**

# A NOTE FROM JOSIE

Dear Friends,

Thank you for reading *A Portuguese Christmas*.

I wanted to write a sweet holiday romance in a unique place, and set *A Portuguese Christmas* near the town of Peniche, Portugal, because the heroine, Krystal Walters, is a world-class surfer. As a non-swimmer, I was fascinated by the skill it takes to surf.

The hero, Adolfo Silva, is an olive farmer. In my research, I learned so much about olive farming and have a great respect for the expertise, patience and perseverance that goes along with a successful olive harvest.

Set against the lushness of beautiful Portugal, it is my hope that you learned some new traditions and celebrated the wonderfully festive Portuguese holiday along with me and the characters.

If you loved this sweet romance as much as I loved writing it, please help other people find *A Portuguese Christmas* by posting your amazing review, as well as for the bundle: Holiday Hearts Volume 1.

A Portuguese Christmas is available in ebook, paperback, Large Print paperback, Hardcover, and audiobook.

I'd love to meet you in person someday, but in the meantime, all I can offer is a sincere and grateful thank you. Without your support, my books would not be possible.

As I write my next sweet or inspirational romance, remember this: Have you ever tried something you were afraid to try because it mattered so much to you? I did, when I started writing. Take the chance, and just do something you love.

Happy Holidays and *Feliz Natal*!

Spotify Play List Here.

With sincere appreciation,

Josie Riviera

Love sweet and inspirational romance holiday stories? Be sure to check out these book bundles:

Holiday Hearts Volume 1
    Holiday Hearts Volume 2
    Holiday Hearts Book Bundle Volume Three
    Holiday Hearts Book Bundle Volume Four

# A TRADITIONAL PORTUGUESE CHRISTMAS RECIPE

**Bacalhau A Braz (Dried Cod Dish)**

5 Large potatoes
3 pieces of boneless, skinless dried cod (previously soaked for 24 hours)
4-5 jumbo eggs
3 large onions
4 large garlic cloves
1/3 cup half and half or whole milk
oil to fry potatoes
salt, pepper, paprika to taste
½ cup olive oil

The salted dry cod needs to be presoaked inside a pan with water, in refrigerator, for 24-36 hours. If cod has been pre-soaked and is frozen, boil for 5 minutes to defrost it.

Cut the potatoes into fine sticks (as close to shoestring as possible) and sprinkle with salt. Fry potatoes in hot oil and put aside.

In a large pot, place the olive oil and sliced onions. Cook onions until transparent. Add cod broken into small pieces (about the size of your fingers) and chopped garlic. Cook for about 10 minutes, stirring occasionally. Add the eggs (that have previously been beaten with half and half) alternating with the fried potatoes and mix well. Add salt, pepper and paprika to taste.

To serve, place in a platter and garnish with fresh parsley and olives. Serves 6.

Enjoy!

# ACKNOWLEDGMENTS

An appreciative thank you to my patient husband, Dave, and our three wonderful children.

# ABOUT THE AUTHOR

Josie Riviera is a *USA TODAY* bestselling author of contemporary, inspirational, and historical sweet romances that read like Hallmark movies. She lives in the Charlotte, NC, area with her wonderfully supportive husband. They share their home with an adorable shih tzu, who constantly needs grooming, and live in an old house forever needing renovations.

To receive my Newsletter and your free sweet romance novella ebook as a thank you gift, sign up HERE.

Become a member of my
   Read and Review VIP Facebook
   group for exclusive giveaways and FREE ARC's.

josieriviera.com/
josieriviera@aol.com

# A SNOWY WHITE CHRISTMAS (A SWEET CONTEMPORARY ROMANCE) PREVIEW

Sometimes Margaret Snow's guilt would go away for a few minutes. But it always returned. Insistent. Dull. Intense.

She was a terrible mother. Check.

She'd never amount to anything. Check.

She only thought about herself. Check.

These negative thoughts chattered incessantly, tucked ever so slightly behind everyday activities. Like uncaged wild animals waiting to pounce at the first opportunity.

She glanced out her office window. Despite the wind and ice, city workers were adding cheery red bells and silver holiday trimmings to the streetlights. It didn't help. November in upstate New York promised gray skies, bitter sleet, and not an ounce of cheeriness until spring. Today was no exception.

What was the weather like in California? She checked the weather app on her phone. As expected, sunny skies in Los Angeles were predicted throughout the Thanksgiving holiday.

"Unbelievable," she whispered. "How could two places be so different?"

And why was she stuck in the lesser desirable of the two?

It was her own fault. She'd forgotten her lines during her last audition because she'd been preoccupied with her daughter's insistent cough that had lingered for weeks. But her agent, Sid, and the casting director hadn't been interested in excuses, and they just dismissed her as a wannabe actress who didn't take the acting profession seriously.

"Stick to modeling," they'd said.

She sighed. She'd been back in her depressing hometown only three weeks and already felt limp and exhausted.

But her daughter Amelie seemed content, and only Amelie mattered. Margaret grinned, remembering the impish smile Amelie would flash whenever she had rolled round and round on their favorite California beach. She'd emerge covered in sand, her small eyeglasses placed carefully on a nearby towel. Her incessant coughing spells would follow, but the physician assistant she saw assured Margaret this was normal in a frail child, and as long as

Amelie didn't develop a fever, there was no need for concern.

"See? I'm fine, Mom," Amelie would say, giggling while demonstrating a perfect cartwheel in the sand. "Now let's go for peppermint ice cream."

Margaret's heart did a funny little turn. Amelie was so much like her father. A perfectionist and a planner. And that was why she'd ensured that Amelie would never know him.

Grumpy, her African grey parrot hanging upside down from the top of its cage, chirped an out-of-tune melody.

"Talk. Say something," she said, knowing he couldn't hear her.

He stared back and shook his head.

She sipped her cup of cold black coffee and shuffled through the stack of blank applications on her desk. The famous actress she'd hoped to become was now relegated to this, a talent agent looking for talent in a town that had none. So demeaning, but at least she was able to provide for her daughter. She sighed, louder this time, twisted the wadded-up handkerchief on her lap and dabbed at her eyes.

A familiar Christmas carol played faintly on the radio, an instrumental arrangement of "Jingle Bells." Shouldn't there be a law prohibiting the playing of Christmas music before Thanksgiving? She clicked it off and gazed absently at the cornucopia wreath tacked lopsided on her office door. Her office was a mess, with boxes piled in a far corner, but she'd only been in Owanda a few weeks and hadn't had time to unpack.

A loud knock brought her attention to the present. Lucy, Margaret's best friend since childhood, opened the door. "Are you busy? You are, right?" She blinked twice, the signal they'd devised years ago for impending disaster.

"Should I be?" Margaret stuffed the handkerchief into her skirt pocket and set the coffee cup on her desk. Formalities weren't observed in upstate New York. One simply rapped on the door and barged in because everyone was considered family. But the only family she'd known lived in a fairy tale. No mother had ever bounced her on her knees or sung lullabies at night. Her mother had been too busy hiding from her drunken, violent husband.

"One of your elves is here for his interview." Lucy actually said this with a straight face. Her blonde hair was styled into an angled bob, soft wisps cascading around her broad cheekbones. She never left the house unless she looked picture-perfect, even if she was only heading to the grocery store. Hollywood had changed her. It had changed them both.

"I tried to stop him, but he knows us too well." Lucy stepped closer and cupped her hands around Margaret's ear. "And take my word, he really knows *you*."

Sure he did. Margaret felt the scowl settle on her forehead. She'd been a swimsuit model, and men had excellent memories when it came to bikinis and the women who filled them. She'd never modeled topless—never. But skimpy? Well ... yes, if it paid the bills and Amelie's tuition. And this elf could request her autograph with a gold pen and silver paper, but he'd be leaving her office empty-handed.

Lucy shook her head. "He was always so demanding."

He was always ...

"Send him in," Margaret replied. She'd dealt with pushy fans before. He could take his autograph book and—

But he'd already barged into her office, all six feet of charm. He was, after all, from upstate New York. See above if you forgot.

With a wave as if she were leaving for a trip abroad, Lucy said, "I'm in my office if you need me." She retreated into the hallway and closed the door.

"My lovely princess," he was saying, "you're as beautiful as ever." He glanced at the parrot. "And I see some things never change. Your house always resembled a pet hotel."

She gaped, stunned by the deep voice and all-too-familiar endearment.

She caught her reflection in the mirror on the opposite wall. "Mirror, mirror, who's the fairest?" he'd always teased. She wasn't beautiful, but her cheekbones were high and her skin smooth and clear. The rest of her had been gangly arms and legs and too-dark eyebrows.

Was she sitting or standing? All the poise and modeling classes were forgotten in the space of a second. Fernando. Fernando. Fernando. It couldn't be, not after all these years. She drew in a breath and held it.

He brushed a hand through his dark hair, dampened from the icy weather. "I heard you were back in town."

She swallowed. How did a man look so put together in this type of weather? Her voice returned and matched her shaking body. "You live in Owanda?"

"I thought I did, although you're making me question it." He looked around, a slight smile gracing his mouth. "Remember we lived two blocks from each other?"

Except she'd lived in the double-wide trailer at the edge of a trailer park and he'd lived in a cozy bungalow with white shingles and a red front door. She looked off for a moment, needing to focus on something else, anything else. Grumpy appeared to be sleeping.

"How could I ever forget?" she asked.

Fleeting hurt dimmed his gaze, but the smile remained. "You forgot quickly, actually." He took a step forward, seemed to think better of getting closer, and halted. "I've missed you." He glanced at the parrot. "Don't tell me, let me guess. He's blind."

"Deaf."

"Does he talk?"

159

"No, but sometimes he sings off-key." She looked pointedly toward the street. "Probably because he's speechless at the terrible weather."

Fernando laughed. "It's not so bad here. Summers are very pleasant."

It took everything in her to remain calm and silent. He was digging in for more conversation, offering small talk before he began his interrogation.

"I brought you a gift." He retrieved a small box, wrapped in gold foil paper with a silver bow, from beneath his wool coat and held it out to her. "Welcome home."

"Thank you, Fernando, but this isn't home." There. She was able to say his name aloud.

When they'd been together, he'd always surprised her with little wrapped gifts—her favorite drugstore perfume, technical books about nursing injured animals, a small leather journal for her notes. Inside the package he'd always write in his bold, neat script: "To my snow white princess, all my love."

"And I can't accept any gifts," she added.

"Of course, you can." His dark brown eyes gleamed with a certainty that she would, indeed, accept it. He carried his belief confidently on his muscular shoulders that life around him went according to his plans. He hadn't changed.

"No, I can't." She pushed back her chair so quickly, it clattered to the floor. Gracefulness had never been her forte and, yes, she'd been sitting. Fortunately, the falling chair gave her something to do—scramble and bend to retrieve it, taking longer than necessary because frustration and memories collided. When she stood, she held the chair upright in front of her like a lion tamer. She'd read a magazine article that a lion tamer used the chair in the ring to confuse the lion, not as a form of defense. All she needed was a whip in the other hand, but the same article had assured that the tamer's whip was only for show. So she stood face to face with Fernando, holding a useless chair and a non-existent whip that wouldn't have helped anyway. Tanned and attractive, he watched her with desire in his gaze. He resembled a sexy magazine ad for a man who desperately needed a shave and didn't care.

He moved her small Christmas tree to the corner of her desk, then placed his gift on the opposite corner. "Please. I bought this especially for you many years ago."

"What are you doing in my office?" Not waiting for a reply, she turned and placed the chair behind her. Swiveling back, she smoothed her lemon-colored skirt and focused on the framed photo hanging on the opposite wall. In the photo she was arm in arm with a famous male actor, and they both held a glass of champagne. Her silk dress was low cut, inappropriately tight, and beyond short. What had they been toasting? She couldn't remember. Her hazel eyes in the photo stared back, glassy with too much drink. Her gaze darted to Fernando. His smile had changed, now slow and insolent as if he'd read her mind and agreed she'd been too provocatively dressed for a twenty-year-old girl. The gleam in his eyes was gone, and he'd reverted to his default setting of disapproval, one of his favorite settings. She'd never met his expectations of the cloyingly cute, content upstate New York girl.

"I thought you lived in Los Angeles," he said. "That swimsuit photo shoot you were in for the sports magazine was the main topic of conversation in this town for several weeks. You and that minuscule yellow bikini made the cover."

"I do. I did. What did you say you're doing here?" She braced both hands on the edge of her desk. Her palms were sweating. What was the advice when confronted with an uncomfortable situation? Stay calm and imagine the other person naked. Yikes! That didn't work as images of his naked, muscular body flooded her senses. She inhaled so loudly, the sound filled the stark room. As she fingered the wadded handkerchief in her skirt pocket, her gold bracelets jingled with a busy clink, reflecting her agitation. Lazy afternoons in his bed when they'd ducked out of high school early were forever seared into her brain. Years of therapy obviously hadn't helped. One minute with him and she reverted to a flustered schoolgirl.

An impish grin moved across his face.

"I'd heard you'd moved out of the area and worked in Florida for some real estate company," she said.

"Don't believe everything you hear. I'm back and forth." His gaze lingered on the top buttons of her blouse. "I'd read in one of the tabloids you were considered for a leading role in a Hollywood adventure film."

She stiffened. "Don't believe everything you read."

Rejection was part of the acting business. Her agent had explained that the role had ultimately been given to a younger upcoming actress who'd worked in classical theater. "Things will pick up in January," he'd assured her.

Fernando shook his head. "An adventure film doesn't seem suitable for an actress with your talent. You probably would've been running around scantily clothed while the action took place all around you." His tone held kindness and understanding. "Besides, the role was for a blonde, and you wouldn't want to change your hair color again. You're stunning when you're a brunette."

"Thanks. I'll be sure to pass your opinion on to my agent." She resisted the urge to touch her hair and shuffled the applications on her desk instead.

"Are you in Owanda for a couple of days visiting friends?"

*Please be here for a short while. Like one day.* In the meantime, she calculated how long it would take to pack her and Amelie's suitcases and leave town. Two days, maybe three.

And how would Amelie adjust to the news? Today was her first day at a reputable public school for the deaf and things were settling into a new normal. Margaret squeezed her eyes shut for a moment. She needed this job to buy back her trailer. She needed a big break in Hollywood so that Amelie could return to her private school. She needed to get out of this decrepit town if Fernando was here.

His gaze had taken permanent residence on the low neckline of her green blouse. "No friends you'd know." He loosened the wool scarf around his neck and turned to the window, a look of feigned surprise on his face. "So you're gracing us with your famed presence because you'd prefer to interview elves rather than star in million-dollar movies or appear on the covers of magazines? Are the paparazzi camped outside? I don't remember seeing any."

"They couldn't work on their suntans in upstate New York."

"Are you visiting anyone special for Thanksgiving? Your parents passed away a few years ago."

Probing, as usual. Leave. Please leave. Don't ask any more questions.

She swallowed. "Yes, both my parents are gone." Always, the sorrow she should've felt wasn't there.

Sadness blurred his striking features and tiny lines creased his forehead. His face showed his thoughts like a road map, although the road map looked more mature and a tad worn. Perhaps he'd aged as much in six years as she had.

"I'm sorry for your loss," he was saying. "They weren't perfect, but I believe they loved you very much."

"They didn't, but thanks." Her throat ached at the recollection of the childhood whippings she'd endured at the hands of her father while her mother sat silent.

"You're still a woman of few words," he said.

"Who's interviewing whom?"

"Just like old times. I talked and you responded in mono-syllables. I never knew what you were thinking."

She shifted. "Why are you here again?"

He unbuttoned his long gray wool coat. The sable-black scarf hung loosely around his neck. "Don't you know why?"

"No, I don't, but if this is a game and I'm supposed to guess, then I'll change the subject to the weather because I'm not good at guessing." She glanced at the clock. Still time to make an escape from his certain interrogation. "How's this? I haven't experienced a white Christmas in a long time."

"I only returned a few months ago, but I imagine the winters are as harsh as ever," he said.

"So you live in Florida? The weather is warm and sunny there."

"I didn't say for certain, but I appreciate you trying to check up on where I live." That seemed to please him, and a smile appeared. "You looked surprised when I walked in."

Surprised? Talk about understatements. An eye roll was in order, but he was watching too closely. She stood straighter. "You mean when you barged in. And yes, you were the last person I ever expected to see again."

"After high school graduation, there was nothing left for me, so I left the area," he said.

"You always said you liked this depressing, freezing town."

"Owanda is comfortable and familiar, but it wasn't the same without you."

*Because you disappeared without a word.* He didn't say it. He didn't have to. His road-map features showed anger, then hurt. Why couldn't he hide his emotions? All the men in Hollywood said one thing while meaning another. But they were actors and agents, and he was an open, honest canvas. Right and wrong. There was no gray area for him.

"You know I needed more than what Owanda offered," she said.

"Certainly more than I could ever offer."

The gentleness in his voice was unexpected, and the shock she'd felt when he entered was draining away to something else. He'd offered her caring and security. And love.

She suppressed a rush of sudden tears. "I've never been satisfied. I wanted more than a Saturday night at the local movie theater followed by a keg party."

"A woman as lovely as you wanted something better than a guy from a small town who spent his nights partying."

"You were popular. Hockey team, class president, you managed it all."

He smiled. "I was always true to you."

His smile was so genuine, she returned it. "I know you were."

They were allies for a moment. But if he suspected she was hiding anything, he'd board the truth train and never get off. She snapped her thoughts away from panic and inhaled a steadying breath. He'd never know. He'd never know.

He held up his hands, palms out, a gesture of understanding. "I'm not asking for an explanation for why you left. I've never analyzed people's motives nor judged them."

"You've always been the better person."

When you weren't drinking.

He dropped his hands. "So you decided to leave sunny Los Angeles to work for your former talent agency at the coldest time of the year and interview elves?"

"It's temporary. I'm between jobs and doing my agency a favor."

She was desperate.

"Plus," she continued, "this allows me an opportunity to spend the holidays in an authentic winter setting to research my next role as a snow princess in Alaska. Of course, the screenplay is only in the planning stages." She glanced at him, hoping he actually believed her story. He seemed relaxed, his expression suggesting interest. Perhaps she was a better actress than her agent thought.

He nodded. "The weather doesn't get any more wintry than upstate New York."

"For this current project, my agency has asked me to audition men four feet ten inches or shorter for jobs at the mall as Santa's helpers." She glanced at the neatly wrapped package on her desk. "If you're trying to bribe me with a gift to get a job ..." She gazed up at his tall, lean frame and gave a rueful laugh. "Sorry. You don't fit the role requirements."

His gaze locked with hers, a wry smile on his lips. "Actually, I'm here to represent my twin brother, Michael. If you recall, he's a dwarf."

She nodded slowly. "Of course. I'm sorry, I'd forgotten about him."

Years ago, she'd enjoyed weekly Sunday dinners at Fernando's home. Michael had worn a hearing aid because the bones in his ears were so small, but the Brandts' good-natured teasing and shouting made up for any hearing impediment. She'd learned sign language because of Michael. Ironic, as signing was one of the main forms of communication she used with Amelie. The remembrance of mouthwatering sausages, green vegetables, and sauerkraut simmering on the Brandt kitchen stove teased her nostrils. His mother was Spanish—hence Fernando's Spanish name—but had cooked German food to please her husband.

Margaret had sworn off German food after leaving Owanda because it brought back too many memories. His family had been so demonstrative, so caring, so unlike her own. Her mother had never cooked a hot meal. In fact, she'd never cooked any meal. And Margaret had had only two conversations with her father in her entire life. Both times he'd been sober. Two times, in eighteen years.

Fernando's mother had always sent Margaret home with leftovers in case there wasn't any food in her house. There never was.

She cleared her throat. "I didn't advertise for dwarfs."

"You advertised for elves, but dwarf is a politically correct term. Michael can be Sneezy today because he's coughing and having chest pain. However, I took him to our family physician, and he's fine." Fernando smiled. He had those crinkly laugh lines around his eyes she remembered so well. "Now you only need to find six more dwarfs. What were their names again?"

She held up a hand. "Thanks, I know the names of the seven dwarfs. And I'm looking for elves, not dwarfs marching off to a mine every morning."

"The dwarfs were searching for diamonds. Some were kept and some were discarded, but all diamonds are rare and precious." He gave her a long, appreciative look and then glanced at the applications on her desk. "The economy didn't recover here as well as it did in other parts of the country. Most people in our town will take any job available."

*Our town.* Owanda was his town but it certainly wasn't her town. She was a California girl now.

She offered him an application and pen. "I need to leave soon, so you can mail it back to the agency. The address is at the top."

"This won't take long." He grabbed the pen and pulled a chair up to the opposite side of her desk. He shrugged off his coat and scarf, slung both behind the chair, and sat. His absorption in the application gave her time to retuck her blouse into her skirt and quickly feel that all the buttons were securely fastened. She lifted her chin and offered an in-control smile just in case he looked up, hoping she gave the appearance of a self-confident movie star. If only she could wipe away the sweat gathering beneath her fringe of bangs without looking insecure.

She glanced at the clock. Two fifteen. Amelie was dismissed from school at three o'clock.

He pushed the application toward her, along with the business card he recovered from the pocket of his well-tailored gray suit. "I'll give you one of my cards."

"Thanks." She stuffed the card into the top drawer of her desk without looking at it, along with his gift.

He quirked a dark brow but said nothing.

She perused his neat handwriting on the application, instantly recognizable even after all these years. Her mother had forwarded his unopened letters to California. He'd written her love letters pleading with her to return. He'd admitted he had an addictive personality and vowed to give up drinking.

She never answered him. At eighteen years old and pregnant, the bright lights of Hollywood were a beacon for a wealthy new life she could achieve on her own merit. She was an independent woman who relied on no man.

She studied the application. "Your brother still lives at your old address?"

Fernando loosened his navy tie. "Yes."

"With your parents?"

"Sadly, my father passed away several years ago. Michael lives with my mother, although he had his own apartment for several years. Lately he's prone to seizures, and I insisted he no longer live alone. He's also recovering from a major operation."

"I'm sorry. I hope he's up to working."

Fernando's gaze drilled into hers with a silent plea. "Work is the best therapy for his recuperation, and it will take his mind off his ailments. Nothing like being an elf in the world of make-believe to forget all your cares."

A beat passed.

"Without dreams, life would be boring and empty," she said.

"Keep your head in the clouds if you want to, but your feet should be firmly on the ground." A deep smile emphasized his dimple. He hadn't outgrown the light sprinkling of freckles on his nose and cheeks. He'd been the best-looking guy in the senior class, rugged and lean, his T-shirt worn untucked. He'd offered her love, but now something else simmered beneath the surface, a resolve edged with tenacity.

He studied her face. "This is the point where you're supposed to press me for details about my life."

She offered him an indifferent shrug. He returned the shrug. A shrug contest. Who could act the most disinterested?

"All right, if you're not interested in me, let's talk about Michael." He leaned back in the chair and crossed his arms. "Do you have any information regarding the job? That is, if you decide to hire him."

She grinned. "There's a shortage of elves in Owanda, so he's got the job. The local mall is setting up a Christmas display in its center court and needs several elves to assist Santa while the children wait in line to see him." She scanned the application. "You listed Michael's phone number and e-mail, so I'll contact him directly. The job will begin the day after Thanksgiving and end Christmas Eve. I hope he's prepared to work nights and weekends, because Christmas isn't all fun and games."

"Of course it is." His dark eyes were filled with warmth again. "I love Christmas."

Snowball fights in the Brandts' backyard. Multi-colored lights and silvery tinsel decorating the Christmas tree, the scent of fresh pine in their living room. The savory aromas of almond crescents and cinnamon stars wafting from the warm kitchen.

Her own childhood house with no Christmas tree, broken lights permanently strung along their front porch, and a drunken, drug-addicted father permanently strung out on the living room couch.

She chewed her bottom lip, a habit from childhood. Her voice softened. "Christmas isn't joyful for many people."

"You and I used to laugh together, sometimes over the silliest jokes. You loved holidays, especially Christmas."

"I'm an aspiring actress. Maybe I was pretending."

He shook his head. "I know you well. Very well. You weren't acting."

She waved a hand dismissively. He was watching her too closely. "Christmas is for children."

"Christmas is for everyone." His voice had a slight catch, but perhaps she imagined it. "Nothing is more precious than seeing a child's face on Christmas morning and the assurance everything's right in the world."

His words almost finished her. Tears sprang to her eyes. There wasn't room in the air for shiny expensive gifts and high expectations. The clock on the wall ticked the minutes, hours, days. Only forty days until Christmas. She'd never be able to stay in Owanda if he were here. She straightened her shoulders and met his probing stare, reminding herself she was not the destitute, dependent girl she'd once been.

End of Excerpt *A Snowy White Christmas* by Josie Riviera
\*\*\*

Want more? Keep reading A Snowy White Christmas.

# ALSO BY JOSIE RIVIERA

Seeking Patience

Seeking Catherine (always Free!)

Seeking Fortune

Seeking Charity

Seeking Rachel

The Seeking Series

Oh Danny Boy

I Love You More

A Snowy White Christmas

A Portuguese Christmas

Holiday Hearts Book Bundle Volume One

Holiday Hearts Book Bundle Volume Two

Holiday Hearts Book Bundle Volume Three

Holiday Hearts Book Bundle Volume Four

Candleglow and Mistletoe

Maeve (Perfect Match)

A Love Song To Cherish

A Christmas To Cherish

A Valentine To Cherish

A Christmas Puppy To Cherish

A Homecoming To Cherish

A Summer To Cherish

Romance Stories To Cherish

Romance Stories To Cherish Volume Two

Cherished Hearts Six Book Volume

Aloha To Love

Sweet Peppermint Kisses

Valentine Hearts Boxed Set

1-800-CUPID

1-800-CHRISTMAS

1-800-IRELAND

1-800-SUMMER

1-800-NEW YEAR

The 1-800-Series Sweet Contemporary Romance Bundle

Irish Hearts Sweet Romance Bundle

Holly's Gift

A Chocolate-Box Christmas

A Chocolate-Box New Years

A Chocolate-Box Valentine

A Chocolate-Box Summer Breeze

A Chocolate-Box Christmas Wish

A Chocolate-Box Irish Wedding

Chocolate-Box Hearts

Chocolate-Box Hearts Volume Two

Chocolate-Box Double Hearts

Recipes From The Heart

Leading Hearts

New Year Hearts

SENIOR HEARTS

Summer Hearts

Christmas in the Air (1-800-Book)

A Very Christian Christmas

Most books are available in ebook, audiobook, paperback, Large Print paperback and Hardcover.

Many are FREE on Kindle Unlimited!

www.ingramcontent.com/pod-product-compliance
Lightning Source LLC
Chambersburg PA
CBHW071239250626
47163CB00001B/241